The Crocodile

Mary Anning knew that people thought she was odd, spending all her time on the beach digging for fossils. After all, this was Lyme Regis in 1811, and her behaviour was most un-ladylike! Even her friend Geoffrey laughed at her, when he wasn't too busy looking for French spies. However, both children were suddenly rewarded in their search, in the most dramatic and unexpected way . . .

John Tully is the author of several children's novels, including *The Glass Knife*, also published by Beaver Books.

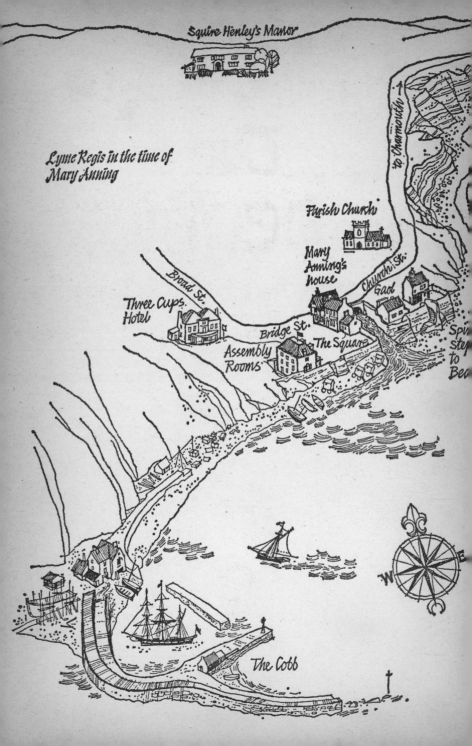

Black Ven   Charmouth

Where the
Crocodile
was found

The
CROCODILE

John Tully

Illustrated by Clifford Bayly

Beaver Books

First published in 1972 by
The British Broadcasting Corporation
35 Marylebone High Street, London W1M 4AA

This paperback edition published in 1977 by
The Hamlyn Publishing Group Limited
London · New York · Sydney · Toronto
Astronaut House, Feltham, Middlesex, England

Printed in England by Cox and Wyman Limited
London, Reading and Fakenham
Set in Monotype Bembo

Contents

Chapter One

Stranger from the Sea

It was after midnight when Sappho flung her nose up in the air and began to howl. No one ever knew why she made such a din that night. The straw in her kennel was fresh and dry. She could have stayed curled up in it, fast asleep like everyone else at the Manor House. But no. . . . Her voice rose and fell in a dismal wail.

Geoffrey Turnstall was a light sleeper. He often woke in the night coughing because of his bad chest. Sappho's howls were more than enough to rouse him. He put his hands over his ears but the noise came through. Was someone torturing the poor dog? There was no other sound in the house. Geoffrey climbed out of bed and dressed quickly.

Geoffrey hurried down to the hall and took his cloak from the closet. He knew he must not go out in the cold without it. He felt better with it wrapped around his thin body.

He let himself out of the house by the front door and went around the side. He opened the yard gate. It was the chance Sappho had been waiting for. Her large woolly body slid past Geoffrey's legs and went bounding off into the darkness.

Geoffrey swung round in a panic and yelled, 'Sappho!'

He caught a glimpse in the moonlight of honey-coloured fur moving swiftly up the lane and set off in chase.

A good run over rough country was just what Sappho liked. She was heading for the cliffs. Geoffrey stumbled after her, calling in vain. He crossed the turnpike road which ran along the clifftop and knew that he must be close to the edge. He began to walk more carefully. He called and whistled but there was no sign of the dog. He saw the cliff edge only a few feet away from him and stopped. It was then he saw a light moving on the sea far below.

A boat was pulling in towards the beach with some men in it. Geoffrey could see one of them more clearly than the others because he held a lantern. He stood in the prow of the boat, moving the lantern from side to side, slowly, as if signalling to someone on the beach. Geoffrey could not make out his features but he seemed to be tall. He was wearing a top hat and a long black cloak. A white cravat at his neck stood out in the dim light.

Geoffrey went down on his knees and crept forward so that he could peep over the cliff edge down to the beach itself. There was no other light to be seen.

As soon as the boat came near to the shore two of the men jumped waist deep into the water. When the next wave came in they dragged the heavy boat as far as they could on to the shingle. The tall man waited till the wave had fallen back again, then he sprang on to the beach. Another man in the boat handed him a bulky object. A box of some kind? Geoffrey could not be sure.

The tall man came up the beach with his box and his lantern. Geoffrey felt sure he was looking for someone who should have been there to greet him, but no one appeared.

The man looked up at the cliffs. Geoffrey pressed himself

down on his stomach. If he were seen he would surely be in danger! Respectable visitors to Lyme Regis did not arrive under the cliffs in the middle of the night. These men must be smugglers. That bulky object could be a cask of brandy. Suppose one of their friends came along the clifftop . . . ? Geoffrey decided that the sooner he got away the better. He began to wriggle back from the edge.

There was a scraping sound in the coarse grass, then a shapeless form hurled itself on Geoffrey's back. The weight squeezed the wind out of him so that he could not cry out. This was just as well. A cry would have warned the men below. By the time Geoffrey had got his breath back a soft wet nose was nuzzling his neck.

'Sappho!' he whispered with relief.

Sappho gave a yelp in reply and Geoffrey put a hand over her muzzle. Then he grabbed her by the collar and set off as fast as he could for the Manor House.

Geoffrey put Sappho into her kennel. She turned round three times in the straw and lay down, content. He closed the yard gate and went into the house. He ran up the stairs without stopping to take off his cloak. Then he rapped on the door of his uncle's bedroom.

Unlike his nephew, Squire Henley was a sound sleeper. The rapping had no effect. Geoffrey tried thumping with the side of his fist but still there was no answer. He opened the door and went in.

'Uncle,' he called, 'wake up!'

What looked like a ghost arose from the pillows. Squire Henley's white nightcap drooped over his face and his nightgown clung around him.

'What – what is it—?'

'It's me – Geoffrey.'

Henley pushed the nightcap out of his eyes. 'What the devil—?'

'I've seen some smugglers, Uncle! Down on the beach!'

'Smugglers?' His gaunt eyes stared at Geoffrey angrily. 'What are you doing out of bed, boy?'

'I got up because Sappho was howling,' said Geoffrey impatiently. 'She ran away and I followed her.'

'Ran away? She isn't lost, is she?'

'No, no! I've brought her back. But I saw a boat come in to the beach. There must have been five or six men in it!'

Henley's hands clutched the sheets. At last he understands, thought Geoffrey.

'You wake me up in the middle of the night – to tell me that?'

He thrust his face at Geoffrey who took a step back in dismay.

'But of course. . . . Aren't you going to call out the Revenue men? As Lord of the Manor isn't it your duty to—?'

'Don't instruct me in my duty!' snapped his uncle. 'Go back to bed!'

'But—'

'We'll talk about it in the morning. If I don't have a headache. I probably shall. Goodnight, Geoffrey!'

There was no more to be said. Geoffrey went back to his room. At least he had done *his* duty. He and Sappho both slept soundly the rest of the night.

The morning sun was pale, with little warmth in it. The tall man shivered and woke up. He was lying on the beach in the shelter of the black cliffs, wrapped in his cloak. He unwound himself like a cat from a blanket and stood up. He pounded his feet on the sand and flapped his arms to drive out the stiffness. Then he looked along the beach towards the town.

The sunlight gleamed softly on elegant houses at the sea front. At the far end the Cobb jutted out into the sea. For hundreds of years the Cobb had offered shelter to incoming ships. Now there were changes, for this was 1811 and Lyme Regis was growing fast.

It was more than fifty years since a learned doctor persuaded the English that drinking seawater was good for them. It had started a new fashion. People who could afford it went to the seaside for summer holidays. They did not drink the seawater any more. The taste made it unpopular. Instead they had discovered the pleasures of bathing in it. Lyme was one of the towns which had grown with the fashion. More visitors came every year. Lyme people were glad to welcome them – and their money. The townspeople had even paid an expert to test their seawater. He had earned his pay. He had given his opinion that Lyme water was saltier than anywhere else in Britain, which proved it must be more health-giving.

The tall man studied the town carefully. Soon he must make his way there, and find a room where he could stay. But not yet. People would not expect to see a visitor arriving so early in the morning. He drew his cloak around him again and settled down to wait. . . .

Chapter Two

'I'll Make my own Way!'

The town was rising. The sound of hammers came from the shipbuilding yard by the Cobb. One or two visitors appeared to sniff the early air. A cart laden with milk churns rattled down Bridge Street, past the town jail and over the bridge which crossed the tiny River Lym.

The last house in the street was on the corner, facing the Main Square. It was built over a shop. The sign over the doorway said, *Richard Anning, Carpenter.* Everyone knew that Richard Anning would not open his shop that day, or ever again. The carpenter was dead, buried in the Parish Churchyard. He had left a widow, one son and one daughter.

But something was happening in the shop window. Mrs Anning was putting up a notice, so that it faced the street. She was a neat little woman with her hair pinned tidily at the back of her head. She wore a spotless white apron over her long widow's dress.

She unlocked the shop door and came out into the street to see how the notice looked. It was written in careful script: *Mrs Anning is willing to offer clean and respectable apartment to genteel visitor.*

She nodded, satisfied. She had taken a lot of thought over the wording. 'Clean and respectable.' She was sure that few rooms in Lyme Regis would be as clean as hers. Most house-wives did not mind a layer of dust, a few cobwebs or an odd cockroach. Visitors were usually more particular. They were well-to-do people with servants at home, used to well-swept floors and freshly washed linen. They were 'genteel'.

A young gentleman of leisure would be the ideal guest. . . .

Mrs Anning went back into the shop. A bell over the door jangled on its spring as the door was closed. She turned into the little living room.

A girl of eleven sat staring into the empty grate. Mary Anning, like her mother, was small in build and wore a black dress of mourning. She had a tiny oval face with eyes that looked very dark beside her pale cheeks. Her legs were spread out, giving her an awkward look. She sat quite still, except for her fingers which wove in and out of one another.

Mrs Anning spoke as she came in. 'There, I've done it!' she said. 'I've put the notice in the window.'

Mary made no response. Her mother frowned. 'Mary, dear . . . ?' Still no answer. 'You must eat before you go to school.'

Mary shook her head slightly.

'Some milk then?' Without waiting for an answer, Mrs Anning poured the last of the milk from a jug on the table into a cup. Mary took it and held it in her lap. Her gaze went back to the grate.

'Let us pray some respectable visitor will be in need of a room,' said Mrs Anning. 'We have to earn money somehow. Goodness knows your brother can't earn enough to help us.'

Mary's brother, Joseph, was fourteen. He had been at work for a year already, far away in Exeter. He was learning how

to put the coverings on furniture, as apprentice to an upholsterer. Like other apprentices, Joseph was given his food and a bed to sleep in over the workshop.

Though Mary didn't speak, her mother's words made her think deeply. What were they to do to make a living? She knew that her father's savings would not last them long. It was brave of her mother to try to let a room, but even if the room were taken it could only be for a few weeks. The summer was nearly over.

'Do drink it, dear!' Mrs Anning interrupted her thoughts. Mary forced some of the milk down her throat.

Mrs Anning shook her head sadly. 'You worry me, indeed you do! 'Tis not fitting for a girl of your age to sit moping, day after day.'

'Please, Mama, I can't—' began Mary. Then she stopped, unable to go on.

Mrs Anning knew well enough what was in Mary's mind. 'Your father is dead and gone!' she said. ''Tis God's will, and all the fretting in the world won't bring him back again!'

Mary bit her lip. She wanted to cry but she knew it was useless.

Mrs Anning went on in a voice that began to tremble, ''Tis as hard for me as it is for you. I loved him too. Now he's gone, I . . .' She turned away so that Mary should not see her face.

Mary looked up in surprise. It had not occurred to her before that her mother needed comforting too. Mrs Anning looked very frail, for all her plumpness. She needed help. . . .

The sound of a bell reached them from the schoolhouse up the hill.

Mrs Anning gave a quick sniff. 'There's the bell,' she said sharply. 'Be off with you!' She went out of the room and Mary heard her footsteps going up the stairs.

Mary took her bonnet from the hook on the door and tied the ribbons under her chin. She put her cape round her shoulders. As she went out to the street she was still thinking hard. . . .

When Mary reached the school the children were nearly all in the classroom. Dame Edith, the teacher, stood in the doorway. Mary bobbed in front of her, but did not go in.

'Please, Dame Edith, may I speak to you?'

'It is late, child. What do you want?' Dame Edith gave the appearance of being severe, but the children knew better. The cane which so often hovered over their knuckles seldom came down in anger.

'I have to leave school,' said Mary.

She explained as best she could – her father's death, her mother's need of help.

'I must begin to earn my living,' she ended.

Dame Edith tapped her lip with a forefinger. 'Did your mother tell you to say this?'

'No. 'Tis my own idea.'

'Then you must ask her before you decide.'

Mary shook her head sadly. ''Tis the only thing to do. I know it is.'

'But you like school, and you're so quick at learning.'

Mary nodded, but she said, 'From now on I must teach myself as best I can.'

Dame Edith frowned. 'If you leave school, what will you do? Will you go into service?'

Mary shook her head firmly. As the daughter of a tradesman with no money to help her she could become the servant of a well-to-do family. But Mary had no intention of waiting on other people from dawn till dusk, seven days a week with only one afternoon off, for a wage of a few shillings a month.

'Not if I can help it!' She looked up at Dame Edith and

although her voice was calm it was full of determination. 'I'll do better than that with my life. I'll – I'll—' She searched for words and said at last, 'I'll make my own way in the world!'

It sounded very grand. Dame Edith was taken aback. 'Make your own way! Child, what are you saying? A girl of eleven can't "make her own way" in this world!'

'I shall do it!' said Mary. 'I shall find some way, even if I am only a girl!'

Dame Edith felt a slight shiver in her spine. The child sounded so certain it was a little frightening.

Mary spoke again in a curiously grown-up way. 'Thank you for all the things you have done for me. I wish I could stay, but I must go now.' She offered her hand to Dame Edith, like a lady taking leave of the drawing room.

To Mary's surprise, Dame Edith leaned forward and kissed her on the forehead.

'Be careful, Mary. Promise me you'll be very careful . . . not to get hurt.'

Mary bobbed again and turned to the gate. Reaching it, she paused and looked back. How often she had wanted to run out of the schoolroom and never come back again! To be free, to start life on her own account. . . . Now she was doing it she found her heart beating wildly. But there was no turning back. She waved to Dame Edith who raised a gentle hand in reply. Then Mary set off down the hill towards her home.

Squire Henley had a headache, as he had feared. That's what came of being woken in the middle of the night! Perhaps a pipe would clear his head. He went into the library. Sappho was lying on the mat in front of the fireplace. She jumped up to welcome him, and when he had patted her she lay down to catch up on her own sleep. Henley was taking his pipe and tobacco jar from the mantelshelf when he saw Geoffrey in the doorway.

Henley had never seen much of his nephew until two weeks ago. Geoffrey's parents lived in London. Henley did not often go there and they did not visit Lyme. Geoffrey had suffered a bad attack of chest trouble earlier in the summer and it was decided that he should spend a month at Lyme to recover his strength. Henley knew him well enough by now to guess that he wanted something.

'Good morning, Geoffrey.'

'Good morning, Uncle.' Geoffrey gave a slight bow.

'Are you still worried about the smugglers?'

'Well, yes,' Geoffrey admitted.

'Humph!' Henley sat in a large winged armchair and began to fill his pipe. 'It's time you knew the facts of life, my boy. Facts about smuggling, for instance.'

'I know it's against the law!' said Geoffrey.

Henley nodded. 'Oh, yes. It's against the law. But the law says that you cannot seize smuggled goods once they have been carried above the high-water mark. Did you know that?'

Geoffrey laughed. 'In that case, how can you ever stop the smugglers? The law is absurd!'

'Is it?' asked Henley. He reached for his tinder box to light his pipe. 'You know there's a war on, don't you?'

Geoffrey frowned. Of course he knew there was a war on. It had been 'on' since long before he was born, and that was twelve years ago. He could remember the excitement when it was feared that Napoleon Bonaparte might invade England. He used to imagine himself, a child of six, standing on London Bridge and defending it single-handed against the French Army. Napoleon was still Emperor of France and master of most of Europe. The British Army was fighting hard battles in Portugal and Spain.

'What has the war got to do with smuggling?' he asked.

'You know that Napoleon stops goods from coming to Britain from Europe?'

'Yes, of course.'

'Yet we still get goods from Europe, even from France itself – in spite of Napoleon.'

Geoffrey thought for a moment. 'You mean, the smugglers bring them?'

'Exactly! Smuggling is very useful to our country. So you see – the law is not so absurd after all!' He sat back in his chair, drawing on his pipe. 'Did you see what they were bringing?'

'I couldn't see very well. There was something. . . . It might have been a cask of brandy.'

'Let us hope so. A fresh cask of brandy is just what I need.'

Geoffrey looked horrified. 'Uncle! Would you drink smuggled brandy, from the land of our enemies?'

Henley fastened a stern eye on his nephew. 'Napoleon Bonaparte has committed many crimes, but the worst of them is denying good brandy to honest Englishmen! Anyone who smuggles some through has my warmest sympathy!'

Geoffrey raised his chin, hoping it gave him an air of dignity. He strode out of the library, then took his cloak from the closet. A brisk walk down to the beach was what he needed.

The streets were bustling with carts and horses and people as Geoffrey made his way down Bridge Street. He crossed a tiny patch of cobblestones and passed under a stone arch which led to the sea front. He leaned over the sea wall, looking down at the beach moodily. There was a sound of hammering nearby. Every forward-looking seaside resort had its sea walk these days. Lyme Regis, not to be left behind, was building a parade which would run all the way to the Cobb.

Geoffrey decided to take a closer look at the building work. He set off down a set of stone steps which wound down to the beach in a spiral between high walls.

He was half-way down the steps when he came face to face with a man coming up from the beach. The man was about twenty-five years old. He had a thin, handsome face ending in a pointed jaw which gave him a determined look. He carried a bulky travelling case and a storm lantern. He wore a top hat and a long black cloak. At his neck was a gleaming white cravat. . . .

Geoffrey flattened himself against the curved wall. The stranger nodded his thanks as he went past up the narrow steps.

Could it possibly be . . . ? Geoffrey shut his eyes for a moment, recalling the tall man in the boat. Then he set off up the steps again. He saw the man go under the arch and turn left down Bridge Street. Geoffrey followed, keeping his distance so that the stranger would not notice him.

The tall man reached the end of Bridge Street and looked round the square. At last his eye fell on the notice in Mrs Anning's shop window.

Chapter Three

A Room to Let

Mary had returned from school. Mrs Anning stared at her in dismay. 'But you must stay at school,' she gasped. 'All girls of respectable families stay at school.'

Mary knew what was in her mother's mind. People would think they were too poor to send her to school. Well, that was true, so why try to hide it? She said nothing, but put on an apron. It seemed the right way to start a life of work.

Mrs Anning knew it was no use arguing. She had never won an argument with her daughter – or with her husband for that matter.

At that moment they heard the bell jingling over the shop door. Mrs Anning hurried into the shop and found a tall young man standing there.

'Good day, sir,' she said, wondering what he was doing there.

'Mrs Anning?' said the young man. 'I see you have an apartment to offer.'

'Oh, yes!' cried Mrs Anning. 'Yes, indeed!' Her eyes noted the visitor's appearance. She decided he must be a gentleman. A very suitable guest!

Geoffrey came round the corner from Bridge Street and found that the man he was following had disappeared. Then he saw the open door of the shop and drew closer to listen to the voices.

'My name is John Cartland,' the man was saying. He bowed gracefully to Mrs Anning.

Well-mannered too, she thought as she bobbed in reply. 'You are most welcome, sir!'

'I want a room that overlooks the sea. I must insist on that!'

'Oh. . .' Mrs Anning had intended to offer her visitor the best bedroom where she and her husband had slept, but that was above the shop, overlooking the square.

Cartland went on firmly, 'My doctor advised me to get as much sea air as possible – for the sake of my health.'

'Of course. . .' Mrs Anning was afraid she would lose this wonderful chance.

'He can have my room, Mama!' Mary had been watching them from the living room doorway. Her bedroom at the back of the house gave a wide view of the sea.

'That is rather a small room,' said Mrs Anning, doubtfully.

'I am not particular as to comfort, ma'am,' said Cartland, 'and I will pay you well.'

Mrs Anning looked up in relief. Then she remembered that Mary was not a tidy girl and her room must be made 'respectable' before it was shown to the visitor. 'If you will pardon me for one moment,' she said, 'I was not prepared.'

Cartland nodded. 'I will wait, ma'am.'

He put his travelling case on the floor. Geoffrey, peeping through the crack at the back of the door, was just able to see it.

Mrs Anning whispered to Mary: 'Speak to our guest nicely.' She said to Cartland, 'My daughter, Mary!' Then she hurried up the stairs.

'Your servant, sir!' said Mary politely. She tried to curtsy, but she could never do it well. Her legs got twisted and she was in danger of falling over.

Cartland did not seem to notice. He bowed again and gave her a pleasant smile. Mary felt shy in his presence. She reminded herself that she was not a schoolgirl any longer. She must learn to 'make conversation' as grown-ups did.

'Did you have a pleasant journey?' she asked.

Geoffrey leaned closer to the doorway to listen.

'Journey?' said Cartland, as if he had not expected the question. 'Ah – yes. I came on the stage coach from London.'

'The coach stops at Charmouth, does it not?' asked Mary. She knew the coaches to Exeter passed through nearby Charmouth but not through Lyme. It was a matter of great regret to the local citizens.

Cartland seemed taken aback. 'Er – yes. To be sure. I stayed at Charmouth last night, you see. I came on to Lyme this morning.'

Mary looked down at the stranger's well-polished boots. The feet were caked with sand.

'By way of the beach, sir?'

The man's eyes narrowed. When his smile was gone he could look very stern. 'Yes! I walked from Charmouth along the beach!'

'It's very nice along the beach,' said Mary.

He looked at her closely. She was smiling. She was obviously not suspicious of him. He relaxed. 'Yes . . . very nice!'

At that moment Mary noticed that the shop door was still open. She stepped forward and closed it.

Geoffrey took a step back as the door shut in his face. His thoughts chased round his head like white mice in a cage. Why should anyone trudge along the beach with a heavy travelling case? Why not take the local coach which ran from Charmouth to Lyme? Or hire a horse at the inn? Or at least walk along the turnpike road on the top of the cliff?

By now Geoffrey was certain that Cartland was the man he had seen in the boat. But was he really a smuggler? His clothes were those of a gentleman. His travelling case was not a cask of brandy. . .

If Cartland were not a smuggler, what was he up to? He was not an ordinary visitor. He was not in Lyme for the good of his health. Why did he want a room overlooking the sea . . . ?

The answer came to Geoffrey in a flash, and it took his breath away. He hurried round the corner into Bridge Street and ran like a hare for the Manor House. This time his uncle *must* take notice!

Squire Henley sat at his desk in the library checking a list of accounts. Mrs Bell, the housekeeper, stood at his elbow. She was a tall, thin woman with heavy brows that gave her a constant frown.

'One bag of meal . . .' read the Squire and ran his finger to the column of figures. His eyebrows rose. 'Three shillings and sixpence!' he gasped.

Mrs Bell nodded.

Henley shook his head, 'If prices go on rising like this we shall be starving!' He was about to read another item when a knock sounded on the double doors.

A small, dapper man came in. He was dressed plainly but neatly. He held himself upright and thrust out his chin as if to impress everyone with his importance. He bowed.

'Yes, Monsieur Duclair?' asked Henley.

The little man spoke in French, '*Pardon, Monsieur!*' He added in English, 'I require a book, if you please.'

Henley waved an arm towards the bookshelves. 'Of course. Anything you want.' He turned to Mrs Bell. 'I'll check this later.'

She nodded and went out to the hall. She was half-way to the kitchen when Geoffrey burst in through the front door.

'Where is Uncle?'

'In the library, but he's busy and—'

Geoffrey was gone before she could say more.

'What on earth—?' gasped Henley as Geoffrey came to a breathless halt in front of the desk.

'I've seen him again!'

'Seen who?'

'The man on the beach! The one I saw last night. The man who came in the boat!'

Duclair turned from the shelf with a book in his hand.

Henley put his fingers to his forehead. He had a feeling that his headache was coming back. 'I take it you mean the smuggler?'

'Yes!' said Geoffrey. 'That is – no! What I mean is – now I've seen him close to, he doesn't look like a smuggler.'

Henley took a deep breath. 'Then what are you wasting my time for?'

'If he's not a smuggler,' – Geoffrey paused to give his words full effect – 'then he must be a spy!'

'A what!' Henley's spectacles – two tiny lenses in a wire frame – danced on his nose.

'One of Napoleon's secret agents!' said Geoffrey.

'*Mon Dieu!*' cried Monsieur Duclair.

Geoffrey waited for Henley's reply. It came slowly.

'Monsieur Duclair . . .' Duclair stepped forward obediently. 'Since you are Geoffrey's tutor, will you kindly give him a lesson on the dangers of a fevered imagination!'

'I didn't imagine it!' Geoffrey was angry.

Duclair came to his aid. 'If there is a spy, he must be caught and shot!'

Geoffrey gave him a grateful look and went on quickly. 'He calls himself John Cartland. It can't be his real name, of course. He pretends to be a visitor.'

Henley sat back in his chair. 'If we suspected every visitor of spying we should fill the Tower of London.'

'He can't be an ordinary visitor – not if he came in that boat!'

Duclair looked worried. 'A boat, you say? In the night?'

Geoffrey explained to Duclair about his adventure during the night. Duclair turned to Henley again. 'We must know more about this man!' he said firmly.

Henley sighed. 'Where did you see him?'

'He went into the carpenter's shop on the corner of Bridge Street. They have an apartment to let.'

'The Annings' shop . . . ?'

Geoffrey nodded. 'It said "Richard Anning" over the door. He was talking to a young girl and he said—'

'A girl?' Henley leaned forward again. That would be Mary. 'Well, well, if it worries you so much I'll have a word with her – er – some time.'

He meant that he would call at the shop, when he was passing. But Geoffrey was already on his way to the door again.

'Where are you going?'

'I'll see to it!' said Geoffrey, and he was gone.

Henley shook his head helplessly.

Duclair was thoughtful. 'An enemy agent – in Lyme Regis? What would he want here?'

'What indeed?' said Henley. 'Forget about it, Monsieur!' He bent his head over the accounts. 'Enemy agent – poppycock!'

Chapter Four

Meeting on the Ledge

An old kitchen table stood in the Annings' shop. On it was a faded notice which said *Curiosities for Sale*. A number of sea shells were arranged to make a pattern. There were also several grey, stone-like objects. Most of these were long, thin and pointed, but one was twisted in the shape of a tiny spiral.

Cartland picked up one of the pointed stones. It looked rather like a pencil. 'What are these?' he asked.

'We call those ladies' fingers,' said Mary. Then she pointed to the spiral stone. 'And that is a petrified serpent, but it is only a very little one.'

Cartland smiled. The spiral did look rather like a coiled snake with no head. 'Petrified? You mean it's been turned into stone?'

Mary nodded. 'They used to be living creatures a very long time ago, so many people say. Now they're like stones, as you can see. Father called them fossils.'

'Where have they come from?'

'From the beach between here and Charmouth. You find them hidden in the rock.' She took the 'finger' out of his hand and put it back in its place. 'My father set those out. They've

28

not been touched since he died. He used to put the table outside the shop door, and visitors bought them.'

'Is that how your father made a living?'

'Oh, no, sir!' A proud note came into Mary's voice. 'My father was a craftsman. He was a cabinet-maker.' (She always thought it sounded better than 'carpenter'.) She looked sadly round the shop, now almost bare. 'We've sold most of his tools and things.'

She went on quickly, 'He used to go down to the beach nearly every Sunday, looking for these. He didn't go to church very much.' She paused, afraid that the stranger might disapprove. 'He used to take me with him to the beach. We were very happy there. . . .'

She felt tears coming and hurried on again. 'Sometimes he went to the beach on other days, when he should have been at work. Then Mama used to scold him, for wasting his time.'

Cartland smiled gently. 'But it wasn't a waste of time, was it?'

Mary looked up at him. What a splendid man he was, to understand that! 'Oh, no! It was *never* a waste of time!'

'If you'll come this way, sir, please.'

Mrs Anning was calling from the top of the stairs. Cartland smiled again to Mary. He picked up his travelling case and the lantern and went up the stairs.

Mary's fingers ran gently over the table top.

A few minutes later her mother came down again, eyes shining. 'He likes the room! Ten shillings a week, my dear! Just think of that! Such a nice gentleman, too!'

Mrs Anning heaved at the water-pump in the scullery. Spurts of water plopped into a large stew pot. 'What about lace-making?' she called over her shoulder. 'There's a good trade for you. A lot of young ladies earn money by making lace.'

There was no answer. Mrs Anning heaved at the pot and carried it into the living room. She put it on the table where Mary stood, peeling carrots for the stew. Mary's thoughts were far away again and lumps of bright carrot were scattered in front of her.

'Mercy! What are you doing? You're cutting off more carrot than is left to cook!' Mrs Anning took the knife away from her. 'You'd better let me do it. Truly, I never knew such a clumsy girl!'

Mrs Anning peeled the carrots with deft, easy strokes. 'How can you make fine lace if you cannot even handle a knife properly?'

Something inside Mary seemed to snap. 'I don't want to make lace!' she said loudly. 'I don't like housework either! I wish I were a boy! I'd like to be an explorer. I'd like to find new lands in Africa, or the Amazon!'

Mrs Anning felt her legs giving way and she sat down. 'You must be mad! It was your father who put such ideas in your head, I declare!'

Mary turned to her mother, angry. 'No, he didn't! He never suggested—'

'He set you a bad example!' Mrs Anning waved a finger at her. 'Letting you run about the beach, climbing over cliffs like a steeplejack. On Sundays too! When decent folk are in church.'

Mary tightened her lips. She had heard all this before. She turned quickly to the door and took down her bonnet and cape.

Mrs Anning picked up another carrot and sliced it furiously. 'I warned him what would come of it! The child is headstrong,

I said. But he wouldn't listen to me – no more than you do. I might as well save my breath—'

The bell tinkled as the shop door opened. Mrs Anning looked round. Mary had gone.

Geoffrey was coming round the corner from Bridge Street when Mary came out of the shop. He guessed she must be the girl that Cartland had been talking to. She strode past him before Geoffrey could speak.

'Just a minute—' he called.

He hurried round the corner after her. Mary was running along Bridge Street.

Geoffrey ran after her.

Mary went like a hare down the curved steps to the beach, then set off towards the tall black cliffs that swept away towards Charmouth.

Geoffrey was already some way behind when he reached the bottom of the steps. 'Wait, please!' he shouted.

Mary ran without pause. Her russet-brown cape billowed out so that she looked like an autumn leaf, blowing in the breeze. Her bonnet became loose. She tugged at the ribbons as she ran and dragged it off her head. Her hair blew into a tangled mass.

Geoffrey was far behind now. Would the girl never stop? His chest began to ache. He was very short of breath.

Under Black Ven cliffs Mary suddenly turned away from the water's edge. She climbed nimbly on to a wide ledge, formed by fallen rock at the foot of the cliff.

By the time Geoffrey reached the ledge there was no sign of her. He looked round helplessly. He moved forward, stumbling over the uneven surface.

He found her at last, lying in a hollow in the rock. The cliffs at this point must have fallen many years ago for the rock had become coated with a coarse, spidery grass. Mary lay on this rough matting, stretched out, eyes closed, face turned up towards the sun.

Geoffrey found he couldn't speak. His breath wheezed in and out of him like a punctured concertina.

She opened her eyes and sat up at once. 'Who are you? What are you doing here?'

Unable to explain, he sank on the grass beside her.

'This is my place! Go away!'

It was in fact where Mary and her father had often eaten their lunch of bread and cheese after a hard morning's search for fossils.

Geoffrey tried to speak but his voice came out like a groan. He held his chest.

'Are you ill?' she asked.

'I'm ... I'm ... all right.' Geoffrey gasped. 'You run so fast. . .'

She waited while he gained some more breath.

'It's my chest,' he explained.

'Who are you?' she asked again.

'Geoffrey Turnstall ... at your service.' He made a polite gesture with his hand, without rising. 'I'm staying at the Manor House, with my uncle.'

Mary's eyes opened wide. 'Is Squire Henley your uncle?'

Geoffrey nodded. Mary scrambled to her feet and bobbed. 'Beg pardon, sir! 'Tis an honour to meet you!'

He felt uncomfortable as she stood looking down at him. 'You may sit down,' he said. 'Please!'

Mary sat down again. 'If your chest is weak you shouldn't have been running.'

'Neither should you! A girl, running like that! All alone on

a beach!' It annoyed him that any girl, especially one younger than himself, could run faster than he could.

'I came here to be alone,' said Mary. 'I have a lot of things to think about. Why did you follow me?'

Geoffrey remembered his mission. He sat up, trying to look important. 'My uncle would like to speak with you.'

She stared at him, puzzled. 'Squire Henley? Why?'

He chose his words carefully, remembering how his father sometimes spoke of his work at the War Office. 'It is a matter of grave urgency, touching the security of the realm!'

Mary giggled. She did not know quite what the words meant, but the way he said them sounded very funny.

Geoffrey rose to his feet, angry. 'It is not amusing!' he said.

Mary tried to look serious.

'Pray call on the Squire at your earliest convenience!' He marched off along the ledge before she could start giggling again.

Mary watched him go, not quite sure she had heard him rightly. What could Squire Henley want with her? Of course she would have to go. It was rather exciting. She had never been inside the Manor House before. She would have to go home first to get ready.

It was hopeless trying to think of her future just now. She walked back to town slowly, fearing another argument with her mother.

There was no argument. Mrs Anning greeted her in silence. When really annoyed with her family Mrs Anning would not speak at all. Mary was glad. It saved explanations.

When she had eaten, Mary ran up to the room which was now hers. She set about making her appearance as neat as possible. The result was not very good. Her hair refused to become untangled. Never mind, it would have to do. Squire

Henley was known to be easy-going about most things.

At the foot of the stairs Mary paused. She knew she ought to tell her mother why she was going out again. But if Mrs Anning knew her daughter was going to the Manor House there would be a terrible fuss. Hours of combing and grooming! And endless questions which she couldn't answer. 'I'll tell her when I get back,' thought Mary.

Cartland made sure that the door of his room was bolted. He unfastened the leather strap round his travelling case and opened the lid. He took out the spare clothing and other oddments. His fingers felt for a tiny tag at the bottom. He pulled it and the false bottom of the case came out, leaving another space underneath. It contained a pistol, powder and shot.

He took out the pistol and checked it carefully. He pulled the trigger and the flint struck a bright spark. Satisfied, he loaded the pistol and put it in a leather pocket inside his coat.

Chapter Five

At the Manor House

Mary stood for a moment at the gate of the Manor House, admiring the neat garden and the cool grey-stone house. Then she walked boldly to the front door and gave a tug on the iron bell-pull. She heard the bell jangling somewhere inside.

The front door opened and the trim figure of the house-keeper appeared.

Mrs Bell looked down at Mary with distaste. 'What do you want?'

'I've come to see the Squire.'

Mrs Bell frowned. 'Only persons of quality come to the front door!' she said. 'Tradespeople go round the back!'

Mary drew in her breath. She knew well enough that her position in society was 'back-door' rather than 'front-door'. But why should she have to go through life by the back door? She was ready to make a fight for it.

'I've been invited here!' she declared firmly. 'The Squire wants to speak to me.'

Mrs Bell frowned even more heavily but it had no effect. At length she stepped back. 'You'd better come in.'

Mary walked into the house with a feeling of joy. Once in

the hall she felt less sure of herself. It was so big! Bigger than the Annings' shop and living room put together.

'Wait here!' said Mrs Bell as she closed the door. 'And pray do not touch anything. I'll inform the Squire that you're here.'

When Mrs Bell was gone Mary flounced a few steps after her, imitating the housekeeper's stately walk. Then she stopped. This was not the way to behave when you called at the front door!

Slowly she became aware of voices speaking in a nearby room. One of them was Geoffrey's. The other she did not recognise. To Mary's surprise they were not speaking English. She guessed that they were talking in French. She edged towards a pair of double doors, one of which was slightly ajar. She bent close to listen.

'*Minuit sonnait au clocher du village,*' said Geoffrey.

He was sitting in front of an ornate table in the library, his head bent over a textbook. He read the words slowly and carefully.

Monsieur Duclair stood beside him. He waved a light cane to and fro as Geoffrey spoke, as if he were conducting an orchestra. Suddenly he rapped the cane on the table.

'*Non, non, non!*' he said, shaking his head. He repeated the words, pronouncing them correctly. '*Minuit sonnait. . .*'

But Geoffrey was not listening. He was staring at the double doors. He was sure that one of them had opened a fraction wider.

'Again!' snapped Duclair.

'*Minuit sonnait—*' Geoffrey began. Then the door creaked.

Duclair noticed it too. He crossed softly over the deep carpet and pulled the door open.

'Oh!' gasped Mary as she found herself facing Duclair.

'What is this?' he asked.

Mary bobbed. 'I beg pardon, sir.' She looked at Geoffrey. 'It was Mr Turnstall who asked me to come here.'

Duclair turned to Geoffrey. 'Who is this young person?'

Geoffrey got up from his chair. 'It's the girl from the carpenter's shop. She can tell us about the man in the boat.' He explained to Mary: 'This is Monsieur Duclair. He is my father's private secretary.'

'Oh?'

'My father is an official at the War Office in London.'

'A very important official!' added Duclair.

He took a tiny silver box from an inner pocket. He opened it and tipped a few grains of brown powder on to the back of his hand. Then he raised the scented tobacco to his nose and sniffed it.

Mary watched, fascinated. She knew the powder was snuff.

Meanwhile Geoffrey went on, 'Monsieur Duclair helps my father by reading French documents and translating them into English.'

Mary was puzzled. 'If you are a Frenchman, how is it you work in the British War Office?'

'He is on our side,' said Geoffrey. 'He has good reason to be. His family were aristocrats before the French Revolution. His father died on the guillotine. The rest of the family escaped to England.'

Mary shuddered. She had heard of the French Revolution and the noblemen executed.

'So he works for my father now,' Geoffrey continued, 'and he has come to Lyme with me as my tutor. Monsieur Duclair is a Viscount.'

'*Le Vicomte de Grenoble!*' said Duclair grandly as he returned his silver snuff box to his pocket. 'When this upstart Napoleon is defeated I shall regain my lands and my fortune. That is why I must help England to win the war.'

Squire Henley appeared at the door.

'What is all this about?' he asked.

Geoffrey stepped forward. 'I asked her to come here, to tell us about the spy.'

'Asked her here!' Henley was taken aback.

'You said you wanted to speak to her.'

Henley was looking at Geoffrey, annoyed. Mary felt uncomfortable. Perhaps she was not welcome here after all.

Suddenly Henley turned to her. 'It is very kind of you to come, Miss Anning.'

Mary bobbed gratefully.

Henley sat in his chair while Geoffrey once more told the story of Cartland's arrival in the boat, this time for Mary's benefit. He explained his suspicions and concluded, 'I've no doubt about it! He's a spy!'

There was a moment's silence, broken by Mary's laughter. 'Mr Cartland, a spy!' she gasped.

Geoffrey turned on her, furious. 'You think everything is funny!'

No one else was laughing. Mary put a hand over her mouth. 'I'm sorry. But Mr Cartland is not a spy. That's impossible.'

They all looked at her closely.

'Why is it impossible?' asked Duclair.

'Because he's a gentleman,' said Mary, 'a very nice gentleman too.'

Henley nodded. 'I'm very glad to hear it,' he said.

Geoffrey looked at his uncle in amazement. 'Just because he acts like a gentleman, that doesn't prove he's not a spy!'

Henley leaned back and tapped his fingers on the desk. He

was obviously satisfied, and anxious that the subject should be dropped.

Geoffrey turned to Duclair for support, but the Frenchman looked doubtful too. 'Are you quite sure you saw a boat?' he asked. 'Are you sure it was the same man in it?'

Geoffrey hesitated. 'It was dark—'

'How dark?'

Geoffrey lost his temper. 'All right! None of you believe me! But you'll be sorry!' He turned on his heel and marched to the door. There he paused in his most dignified style. 'You'll be sorry when we lose the war!'

He stalked out of the room.

Duclair looked horrified. 'Lose the war! He should not even think such a thing.' He bowed to Henley and followed Geoffrey out of the room.

Henley sighed and looked up at Mary. Then he smiled. 'I sometimes think that one of the fruits of victory will be getting rid of him!'

Mary smiled too. She decided that she liked the Squire. She realised that she ought to take her leave now, but something had attracted her attention.

It was a small round table with a glass top. Under the glass were several 'curiosities' of the kind she and her father so often found on the beach. Greatly daring she went to the table and pointed to it.

'May I look at these fossils?' she asked.

'Of course.' Henley came over to the table and stood beside her.

Mary pointed to a group of long, pointed stones. 'Those are ladies' fingers, aren't they?'

Henley nodded. 'That is the popular name for them. The proper name is belemnites.'

'And there's a petrified serpent!' She pointed to a spiral stone much larger than the one in the shop.

'An ammonite.'

'Belemnites, ammonites. . . .' Mary repeated the names carefully. It was good to know the proper names for things.

She pointed to the ammonite again, 'I know that one. I was with my father when he found it. I think you paid him five shillings for it.'

'So I did. I bought a lot of fossils from him. I've sent the best ones to the museum in London.'

Mary was silent for a moment. She knew that the Squire collected for a London museum, and a thought began to form in her mind. It was a thought so daring that she did not like to admit it right away. . . .

'Would the museum take more of these, if you had them?'

'Indeed they would! It's a great pity there's no one to collect them any more.'

Of course the Squire would not dream of collecting them himself. Gentlemen did not go poking about the beach or climbing cliffs.

Mary turned away from the table and stared out of the library window towards the distant sea. 'If someone else were to find them for you . . . would you pay for them?'

'Gladly,' said Henley, 'but who will do it now?'

Mary felt excitement growing in her as her idea became more and more possible. 'Visitors buy them too . . .' she muttered, more to herself than to Henley.

'What are you suggesting?' he asked.

She did not answer aloud but her thoughts were pounding in her head like waves on the beach. 'If only I could . . . on my own! And why not?'

She swung round to face Henley. 'I want to know about

these things !' she exclaimed. She ran back to the table, pointing to the fossils. 'I want to know everything about them ! Father said they are creatures that are dead and turned to stone. Is it true?'

'It is true,' he said, 'so far as we know. The learned men say they are creatures that no longer exist anywhere on earth.' He took the glass top off the table and took out the ammonite so that they could both look at it more closely. 'These creatures must have lived a long time ago. Longer than wc can imagine. They must have lived in a world we know very little about.'

The words sent a new thrill down Mary's spine. She knew she could never be an explorer in Africa or South America. But here was 'a world we know little about' on her own doorstep – not a mile along the beach ! A world of strange creatures that no one had ever seen. . . .

Henley said, as if he read her thoughts, 'The Lord alone knows what wonders are still to be found.' He put the ammonite back in its place and picked up another stone-like object. This one was about the size of his fist, roughly circular, but knobbly round the edges. 'Take this, for instance. The learned men think it must be part of a very big creature. Part of the backbone – one of the pieces called vertebrae.'

'But what creature is it?'

'No one knows. For want of a better name, some call it the crocodile. Others say it is something quite different – different from anything we know.'

Mary repeated the words softly, on the edge of her breath, 'The crocodile !'

Henley smiled at her. 'Perhaps some day someone will find the mysterious creature, all in one piece.'

In that moment Mary knew what she had to do. If she had to

pull the cliffs apart with her bare hands, rock by rock... If it took her a lifetime...

'Tell me about it!' Her voice was scarcely more than a whisper. 'Tell me about it, please!'

Mary and Henley talked for more than an hour. She asked him to tell her everything he knew about the crocodile. Henley brought out several books which he laid open on his desk.

Mary studied one which showed a drawing of cliffs similar to those at Lyme.

'Is it true that Black Ven cliffs were once at the bottom of the sea?' she asked.

'So they say, but it was a long, long time ago,' Henley answered. He pointed to the drawing. 'If you look closely at the rock face you can see it is formed in thin layers, one on top of another.'

Mary nodded. She did not need a drawing to tell her what she had so often seen for herself.

'Those layers were formed by mud,' Henley went on. 'The mud was brought down by rivers as they flowed into the sea. It settled on the sea bed and built it up, layer after layer. Very slowly, of course. It must have taken many years to form even a single layer.'

Mary's eyes widened. If these tall cliffs had grown under the sea it must have been happening long before history began! The world itself must be a lot older than most people thought.

'If the cliffs were under the sea, how is it we can see them now?' she asked.

'There were terrible upheavals in the earth,' Henley explained. 'In some places land sank under the water. In other places – on this coast, for instance – the sea bed was pushed upward. That is why we see the cliffs out there.' He glanced out of the window.

Mary looked at the fossils. 'And these creatures which are found buried in the rock? How did they get there?'

'Oh, they were creatures that lived in the sea in those distant times. When they died they fell to the bottom and fresh layers of mud kept covering them up. So there they are today, stuck in the rock like currants in a bun!'

'All turned into stone. . . .'

'The soft parts of their bodies disappeared, naturally. But the hard shells or skeletons remained. These bone parts slowly changed into a kind of stone.'

Henley was about to say more when he glanced at the gilded clock on the mantelshelf. 'Heavens! Look at the time!'

Mary looked too, with a feeling of guilt. 'Mama will wonder where I am!'

'You must call on me again,' said Henley.

'Oh, thank you, sir. Yes, indeed I shall – when I have found fossils of my own to show you!'

She had almost reached the door before Henley realised what she had said.

'When *you* have found fossils—!' he exclaimed.

Mary smiled and nodded. 'I know what I shall do to earn money. I shall go down to the beach every day looking for fossils. I know I can find them. Father showed me how. I shall sell them to visitors at the shop. When I have really good ones I'll bring them to you, and you can buy them for the museum. It's much more exciting than making lace.'

Henley was staring at her as if she were some sort of curiosity herself.

'Is something the matter, sir?'

'Go down to the beach! You?'

'Why not?'

'Why not? You are far too young! And it is no work for a woman. On the beach, alone! It is not seemly!'

Henley was only saying what most people would think. But Mary was not to be put off by what anyone thought, not even the Squire himself.

'Mama often says, "There's a first time for everything." I shall be the first woman to look for fossils!'

Chapter Six

'A Spirit on Fire'

Cartland had been watching the Manor House for some time. He stood among tall bushes which lined the lane just outside the gate, so that no one would spot him from the windows.

The front door opened and Mary Anning came out. Cartland drew still further back among the bushes as Mary passed him. He watched her as she hurried down the lane towards the town and wondered what had brought her to the Manor House.

A few minutes later the door opened again. Cartland stiffened as Monsieur Duclair emerged. The Frenchman strode down the lane swinging his cane.

Cartland waited till Duclair was far enough away, then stepped out from the bushes and began to follow him.

Duclair walked down Bridge Street with his nose tilted as if he were too proud to notice the townspeople and visitors passing by. Out of the corner of his eye he saw a tall young man wearing a top hat and a long black cloak.

Duclair paused a moment, thoughtful. Then he set off down the street again. Yes . . . the young man was following him.

At the jail Duclair turned left under the brick arch. He

stopped at the top of the curved steps and leaned on the wall gazing out to sea.

A few moments later the other man appeared a few feet away. He, too, leaned on the wall looking out to sea. Then he spoke, softly: 'The password is Victory.'

After a pause Duclair gave the answer, just as softly. 'The Victory is for France!'

Cartland relaxed. He looked around. People were strolling along the beach below but there was no one close to them.

'*Monsieur le Vicomte?*' he asked.

Duclair inclined his head, pleased by the use of the title.

Cartland introduced himself. 'Captain Peronne, at your service!'

'You are most welcome, Captain Peronne.'

Both men were speaking in French, keeping their voices low. They stared out to sea as if unaware of each other's presence.

'I know you expected me some days ago—' Cartland began. He stopped. A boy came through the archway bowling an iron hoop that clattered loudly on the flagstones.

'It is not safe to talk here,' whispered Duclair. 'I understand you are staying at the carpenter's shop. I will meet you there – tomorrow morning.'

'Very good, Monsieur!'

Duclair turned and strolled back under the arch into Bridge Street. Cartland continued to stare out to sea. There was a faint smile on his lips.

'Child! Are you out of your mind?'

Mary sighed. She had expected this reaction from her mother. 'I know what you're thinking, Mama. Mr Henley said it was unseemly.'

'Unseemly!' Mrs Anning shuddered. ''Tis unheard of! A girl hunting for fossils all alone!'

She had a good deal more to say but Mary was not listening. She went to the dresser and opened one of the drawers. She took out a leather wallet. Inside were several stone chisels of different sizes, a big hammer and a smaller one, and a soft brush. They were the tools her father had used when he searched for fossils. Mary had often handled them herself.

'D'you hear what I'm saying?' cried Mrs Anning.

'Oh, yes, Mama,' said Mary, politely. She was pleased to find that the tools were still in good condition. She wrapped them up and put them back in the drawer.

It was dark now. Mary lit the oil lamp which cast a smoky light over the room.

Mrs Anning went on talking about what was fit and proper for young women, till at last she seemed to exhaust herself, and sat by the fire staring into the flames.

Mary put an arm round her. 'You may be right, Mama. If I am wrong I expect I shall be very sorry for it. But you see, I have to try. I must find out for myself. . .'

There was silence.

'I'm going to bed now. I want to go down to the beach as soon as it is light.' She stopped and leaned forward, kissing Mrs Anning on the cheek. 'Goodnight, Mama!'

Mary went quickly out of the living room and up the stairs.

Mrs Anning continued to stare at the fire. The lamp burned low and the firelight flickered over the walls of the room. Like tiny lightning flashes.

Lightning! That's what had turned Mary's brain! The lightning all those years ago.

It happened when Mary Anning was two years old. Her

father's trade was successful then and a girl of fifteen called Elizabeth Haskins was paid to help look after the children.

One day Elizabeth took Mary to watch a team of horsemen performing in Rack Field. Half the town had turned out to watch the spectacle. There were cheers and applause for the riders and no one noticed the storm clouds gathering till suddenly the rain tumbled out of the sky. There was a rumble of thunder.

People scattered. Elizabeth grabbed Mary in her arms and ran for shelter under a tall elm tree. Two other girls joined them there.

A few minutes later there was a blinding flash of lightning which lit the whole field. Thunder crashed immediately overhead.

When the noise had died, cries of dismay were heard from people sheltering around the field. The lightning had struck the elm tree! All that was left was a blackened stump, charred and smoking. Beside it on the ground lay four bodies. . . .

People came running through the rain. Elizabeth and the two older girls were dead. Many people who were present that day swore that the little child Mary was dead too.

Mrs Anning cried out in horror as they bore Mary into the house. Her tiny body hung limp and her eyes were open, staring.

Then an older woman spoke. Her tone was calm and matter-of-fact while others were weeping. 'Put her into a bath of warm water!' she advised. ''Tis the best way to allay the shock.'

The child did not stir as Mrs Anning heated her large stew pot on the fire and brought the tin washing bath from the scullery.

The old woman stripped the child and Mrs Anning laid her

in the water. There was stillness as if the whole town waited. At last Mary's eyes flickered. She began to cry.

It was not the end of the story. Up till that time, Mary had been a rather dull child. Afterwards she became bright, eager and quick to learn. People swore that the lightning had set her spirit on fire.

All very fine, thought Mrs Anning as she sat in front of the hearth, but a spirit on fire is not easy to live with! Here was Mary, eleven years old, openly defying her – and not for the first time! The girl might be clever, but stubborn too, and full of such strange ideas.

Well, it was all the fault of the lightning. This thought made Mrs Anning feel a little better. At least it was not *her* fault!

But what would become of Mary? Mrs Anning shook her head at the flames. 'Mercy upon us!' she whispered.

Chapter Seven

Hidden on the Beach ...

The next morning Mary wrapped some bread and cheese in a clean cloth, with a flask of water. She took the leather wallet from the drawer and put on her bonnet and cape. As she reached the front door her mother came down the stairs. They looked at one another for a moment.

'Take care, child,' said Mrs Anning, and went into the living room.

Mary did not run along the beach that morning. She had to keep her strength for the day's work. When she reached the place near the ledge where her father had often stopped, she put down her bundle of food. Her eyes were eager as she undid the wallet and drew out a hammer and chisel. . . .

Monsieur Duclair strolled down Bridge Street into the square. He glanced at the Annings' shop as he passed it. Then he crossed the square to the Assembly Rooms which lay along the south side. The back of the buildings overlooked the sea.

The Assembly Rooms were the main meeting place for visitors to Lyme. Here, for a small fee, you could drink coffee and talk at any time of day and for most of the night.

Duclair went into the Coffee Room which looked out over the square. He chose a table beside one of the windows.

A waiter appeared. Duclair ordered a pot of coffee and a newspaper. When these were brought he opened *The Times* and made a pretence of reading it. In fact he was watching the Annings' shop doorway.

It was half an hour before he saw what he was waiting for – Mrs Anning coming out with a shopping basket on her arm.

Duclair rose at once. He left some coins on the table, and tucked the newspaper under his arm. There was a report from the battlefield in Portugal which he was anxious to study.

He paused beside the Annings' door. People were passing but no one seemed to be watching him. Then the door opened behind him. He slipped inside at once.

Cartland, who had opened the door, closed it again and went up the stairs without a word. Duclair followed him.

In the bedroom the two men bowed to one another, briefly, in military fashion.

'I understand you have some papers for me,' said Cartland, in French.

Duclair nodded. 'They were much too valuable to send by a messenger. Messengers are too often caught.'

'So you sent a letter to Paris instead. You asked that a special agent should be sent over to collect the papers.'

'That is right. I explained that I would have to come here, to Lyme Regis. I got a reply saying that the agent would land here on the twenty-sixth of the month.' He eyed Cartland as if accusing him. 'You are almost a week late!'

Cartland answered impatiently. 'It is not so easy to cross the Channel! British ships were watching that night. We had to turn back. We made another trip as soon as it was possible. I looked for you on the beach.'

'Did you think I would be there – a week later? I couldn't go down to the beach every night, not knowing when you would come.'

Cartland nodded. 'I realise that. I was prepared for it. I brought some things in case I was obliged to stay here awhile.' He indicated the travelling case. 'Now that I am here, Monsieur, what about the papers? What are these documents I am supposed to collect?'

Duclair's manner relaxed. 'You may know that I work for Sir Joshua Turnstall at the War Office?'

Cartland nodded.

'Sir Joshua is one of the first officials to receive dispatches sent in from abroad.'

'You get an opportunity to see these papers?' asked Cartland.

'Yes, frequently. I have sent much useful information to Paris over the past five years.' Duclair was proud of his achievements as a spy. 'A month ago I was able to open a batch of documents before even Sir Joshua had seen them. And what do you think, Captain? They were dispatches from Lord Wellington himself!'

Cartland looked suitably impressed.

'I hid them away at once,' Duclair went on. 'No one at the War Office knows yet that they are missing.'

'What is in these dispatches?'

'There are lists giving the number of men available for duties in every division of the army! Lists of arms, too. Artillery, small arms, cavalry horses – everything!' Duclair paused for effect. 'And that is not all! Lord Wellington writes to the Minister giving his plans for next year's campaign!'

Duclair waved his cane as he went on, 'With this information our own army will be able to defeat the British once and for all! I tell you, sir, these papers could help us to win the war!'

Cartland forced himself to remain calm. 'You have done very well, Monsieur. I am sure you will be well rewarded.'

'I hope so !' said Duclair. 'I have been promised, you know, that for my work as an agent I shall be given back my family estates in France ! I have it in writing under the seal of the Emperor !'

'Napoleon will keep his word,' said Cartland. 'It is lucky for us that the British trust you so well.'

Duclair smiled. 'They trust me because they think I am on their side. But I am a Frenchman ! I must fight for France !'

'And your fortune !' added Cartland. 'I must take the papers to Paris at once. Please give them to me.'

Cartland held out his hand as if expecting Duclair to take the papers from his pocket.

'I do not carry them about with me !' snapped Duclair. 'And I am not sure it is safe to give them to you right away.'

'Not safe?'

'You are under suspicion !'

Cartland was taken aback. 'How? Why?'

'That meddling boy ! Sir Joshua's son. He was out on the cliff, chasing a stupid dog. He saw you arrive in the boat.'

Cartland's fists clenched.

'Fortunately his uncle does not listen to him. Like so many people here the Squire thinks the war is something far away that cannot touch him. I pretended to be sympathetic, to find out how much the boy knew. He is a danger to us. When he gets an idea into his head you cannot shift it. He will worry at it like a puppy with a bone. That is why it is not safe to give you the papers – not until the boat comes again, to take you back to France. When do you expect it?'

Cartland hesitated. 'It will be a few days, perhaps a week. It depends when they are able to make the crossing. I have to keep watch for it.' He glanced towards the window and the sea beyond.

Duclair took out the snuff box. The setback in his arrangements made him nervous again. 'I'll give you the papers when the boat comes.'

Cartland frowned. 'If the boat should come one night, before I can warn you . . . ? I ought to know where the papers are hidden, so that I can recover them for myself.'

There was a pause, then Duclair nodded. 'Very well. I'll show you where they are hidden. Today I must go back to the Manor House. The boy must have his lessons as usual. We'll meet again tomorrow. You will follow me along the cliffs.'

'Along the cliffs?' Cartland looked surprised.

'Naturally I put the papers where they could easily be handed over to you in the boat. They are hidden on the beach!'

Mary heaved at a rock too large for her. She managed to push it over to one side. Water seeped into the shingle underneath. She studied the grain of the rock to see if it might be worth hacking with her chisel.

'Hello, there!'

It was a voice calling from the clifftop. She looked up to see Geoffrey looking down at her and waving. She waved in reply. Then she went back to her work.

Geoffrey wandered a few yards farther along the clifftop, till he came to a ravine that cut into the cliff. It offered a steep but convenient slope down to the beach. He slid over the side and began to scramble down the loose shale.

He was not sure why he had come to see Mary. He knew she would be there because Henley had told him: 'That foolish girl is determined to go hunting fossils all on her own.' Geoffrey agreed she was a 'foolish girl'. So why should he bother with

her? The trouble was, there weren't many other children to bother with. A few, among families friendly with the Squire, but they were a dull lot. Mary was not dull. She had an air about her, as if she were enjoying some great adventure, even if she were only picking among the stones on a beach.

He was just recovering his breath at the foot of the ravine when Mary called to him.

'Look! Look what I've found!'

He tramped over the shingle to join her. She held up a fossil. 'What is it?'

'A petrified serpent – I mean, an ammonite.'

'Oh? Is that all?'

'All! It's valuable! I know it's not very big, but it's all in one piece. See – I got it out without chipping it. 'Tisn't easy to do that.'

He turned it over in his hand. 'Very nice, I'm sure.' He gave it back to her. 'I'll race you up the beach if you like. Up to where that ledge juts out. You can run as well as I can,' he added, in case she thought he was being unfair.

She looked at him as a grown-up might look at a child who was in the way. 'I've no time to go racing. I've got work to do!'

'Work?' He spoke the word with contempt.

'Yes, work!' She added with a note of pride, 'I've got to earn my living!'

She marched down to the water's edge and bent to wash the ammonite in the sea.

He followed her idly. She seemed to be playing an absorbing game in which he had no part.

'I can't stay long,' he said. 'It'll soon be time for my lessons.'

'Please yourself,' came the answer.

Geoffrey gritted his teeth. He was angry with her and he knew there was no excuse for it.

'Very well! I'm going now!'

She did not answer. He turned and strode off towards the town.

At midday Mary climbed up on the grassy patch of ledge to eat her bread and cheese. She did not linger over it. Sitting there reminded her too keenly that her father was no longer with her. No matter. She was carrying on the work they had both loved best. She spent the afternoon on the ledge itself, but she found no more fossils.

The tide was coming in and threatening to cut her off from the town when she packed up her tools. She wrapped the ammonite carefully in the cloth which had held her food, together with some shells she had gathered. Visitors might pay a few pence for a handful of pretty shells. The ammonite was more important. If only she could sell it quickly to prove to everyone (especially her mother) that she was not wasting her time! She decided to display it on the table outside the shop as her father used to do.

Mary began to run again when she got near to the town. It was a bad habit, she knew. Unladylike. But running made her feel good.

She ran up the steps and was still running as she passed under the arch – into the arms of a plump lady coming the opposite way. The lady gave a gasp and Mary dropped her cloth on to the flagstones.

'Oh, ma'am, I'm sorry!' cried Mary.

She fell on her knees. The ammonite! Her one precious find! Was it broken? She found it and turned it over in her hands. No. . . It was unharmed! She breathed a sigh of relief.

The lady had recovered her breath and was about to speak her mind.

'I am most sorry, ma'am,' said Mary again, 'I do hope you are not hurt?'

'Clumsy girl! Have you not been taught better manners—?' Then she stopped. She was looking at the ammonite in Mary's hand. 'What is that you have there?'

'It's a petrified serpent, ma'am.'

The lady held out her hand. 'May I see it . . . ?'

Mrs Anning looked at the clock for the tenth time. Had Mary fallen from the cliff? Had the tide come in and drowned her? Might there be cut-throats on the beach . . . ?

At the tinkle of the doorbell she turned hopefully.

Mary burst into the living room. Her apron was smeared all over with the black mud of the cliffs. Her bonnet hung lop-sided over a tangled bush of hair. Her boots were dripping on to the mat. Her face was streaked with mud but her eyes shone with delight.

'I found an ammonite, Mama – and I've sold it! A lady I met on the way back. She saw the serpent and she bought it! Look!'

Mary opened a grubby hand. Lying in her palm were two bright shillings and a sixpence.

'You see? I can do it, Mama! I can do it!'

She flung herself into her mother's arms mud and all. . . .

Chapter Eight

A Fall of Rock

Geoffrey soon tired of watching the workmen building the 'Marine Walk'.

He walked past the bathing huts and found that he was leaving the town, heading once more for Black Ven cliffs. He tried to tell himself that he was not looking for Mary.

She was not to be seen on the beach. It was midday. Geoffrey climbed on to the ledge and he found her in the grassy hollow eating her lunch. She looked very pleased with herself.

'Hello,' she said, 'sit down.'

Geoffrey looked around. He knew better than to soil his breeches on the black rock. An old smugglers' cask stood on its end. Half its staves had been broken away, but it was still solid enough to bear his weight, so he sat on it.

'Would you like some cheese?' asked Mary.

He shook his head. 'You look very happy. Have you found something else?'

Mary nodded eagerly and handed him another fossil she had cleaned. It was the round, knobbly kind. ''Tis one of them verterberries,' she said.

Geoffrey looked puzzled, till it dawned on him. 'Oh, you mean vertebrae!'

'That's right. A verterberry.'

Geoffrey looked at the fossil with more interest. 'It can't be,' he said at last.

'Why not?' She was angry at once.

'It's much too big,' he explained. 'The vertebrae form the backbone of animals. We have them ourselves.' He leaned forward and ran a finger down her back. 'You can feel them, like a row of little knobs down the middle of your back.'

'I know that!' said Mary. 'What of it?'

'Well, don't you see . . . ?' Geoffrey held up the fossil which must have measured four or five inches across. 'If this were only one piece of a backbone, how big would the creature be?' He stretched out both his arms as far as they would go. 'It would stretch for yards! It would be a – a monster!'

'And why not?' She took the fossil from him and held it to her breast as if it were a favourite doll. 'Did you never hear tell of the crocodile?'

Geoffrey shook his head.

'Your uncle told me about it, and he was told by the learned men in London. They reckon that if you put all the bones together, like you were saying, you'd have a huge creature, like a crocodile.'

Geoffrey shook his head again. 'I've seen pictures of crocodiles. They're not as big as that!'

Mary nodded, slowly. 'It's not *really* a crocodile. It's something else, that nobody's ever seen before. Some say it's like a great fish. And others think it might be a gigantic lizard.'

Geoffrey laughed.

She turned to him, angry again. 'What are you laughing at?'

'You laugh at things. Why shouldn't I? How can a creature be a crocodile, and a fish, and a lizard?'

Mary rose to her feet. 'I told you! It's a creature from a different world.' She turned away and looked up at the cliff towering over their heads. 'It's here, somewhere, hidden in these rocks, and some day I'll find it!'

'Find it!' Geoffrey rose too. The dark rocks looked threatening to him. He felt a sudden fear of the unknown. 'I'd rather you didn't!'

She turned back to him, smiling. 'Are you afeared of it?'

'Certainly not!'

'The creature's dead, so it can't hurt you. It's been dead these Lord knows how many years. More than we can count. I'll not be afeared of it – that I won't!'

Monsieur Duclair leaned against a wall near the Cobb watching the fishermen's wives mending nets. Most of the fishing smacks were out at sea on their day's work, but there were still some ships in the little harbour with their sails tightly furled.

'Good afternoon, Monsieur,' said a voice quietly. Cartland had appeared beside him. 'You will show me now where the papers are hidden?'

Duclair nodded without looking round. 'I will lead the way. Follow some distance behind. People must not see us together.'

He moved away and Cartland waited a little while before he began strolling after him.

Duclair walked through the town and out along the turnpike road on the clifftop. It would have been simpler to walk along the beach but there were too many people who might notice them. Once out on Black Ven there would be no one around. . . .

The road had been built well back from the cliff edge, but

the cliffs were constantly crumbling away under the attack of waves and weather. The road was now almost at the edge in some places. Sooner or later it would disappear into the sea.

Duclair headed towards the ravine where he knew he could climb down to the beach. He never reached it. When close to the cliff edge he saw the two children below.

They were walking along the ledge. Mary stopped and knelt, searching for something.

Duclair drew in his breath in dismay. What were they looking for? Could they possibly suspect that the papers were hidden . . . ? Surely not. Yet whether they were looking for the papers or not there was danger they might find them!

The children moved on, right up to the cliff face immediately below. Mary was tapping at the wall of rock with her hammer and chisel.

Duclair knelt to peer over the edge. His fingers curled round a piece of rock and it crumbled in his grip. Beside him was an overhang, jutting out from the cliff face right over the heads of the children below. Without stopping to think further, Duclair brought his foot down on the overhanging section, digging savagely at the matted turf. He felt it loosen under his heel.

Cartland, still some distance behind, watched Duclair stamping on the cliff edge, and wondered what he was up to.

A fragment of rock, loosened from the overhang, clattered down the cliff face beside Mary. It was followed by more tiny bits, like dust. Mary was too intent on her work to notice, but Geoffrey looked up. He saw the overhang above them. He could swear that it was trembling. He cried out in terror as the whole lump of it pitched forward.

'Look out!'

He grabbed Mary by the waist and dragged her backward.

They fell together on the ledge. The mass of rock landed with a thunderous crash on the spot where they had been standing. It shattered into small pieces. . . .

Duclair did not wait to see the results of what he had done. He turned away from the cliff edge and ran back to the road.

Cartland heard the cry from below. He hurried forward to the cliff edge, at the spot where Duclair had been standing.

Geoffrey helped Mary to her feet.

'Oh, thank you!' she gasped. 'Truly we might have been killed.'

Geoffrey nodded and looked up at the cliff again. He was just in time to see Cartland peering down at them over the edge.

'Look!' yelled Geoffrey, pointing.

Cartland stepped back out of sight at once. When Mary looked up there was no one to be seen.

'What is it?' she asked.

'It was *him!*' Geoffrey was still pointing to the clifftop.

'Who? I don't see anyone.'

'Your Mr Cartland! I saw him. He pushed that rock down on top of us. He was trying to kill us!'

Mary looked at him in amazement. 'Mr Cartland? What are you talking about? A piece of rock fell, that's all. Rocks do fall from the cliff. You were wise to look out for it.'

Geoffrey's heart was pounding. Now all his suspicions were confirmed. 'Rocks don't fall on a calm day like this – do they?'

Mary hesitated. 'It's possible. . . .'

'The rocks fall when it rains, when the water washes them down! I tell you that was done on purpose!'

Mary stamped her foot. 'By Mr Cartland? I don't believe it!' She was angry with Geoffrey. 'You have a twisted mind!'

Geoffrey was angry too. 'What do you know about anything? You're only a carpenter's daughter!'

Mary took a step back, deeply hurt, but Geoffrey went on: 'You think you're clever, don't you? Looking for monsters! Well, I'll tell you something – there are no monsters! They don't exist, they never did exist, except in fairy-tales!'

Mary put her hands over her ears but she could not blot out his voice.

'Do you know what you are?' he said. 'You're just a silly little girl, playing silly little games on a beach!'

Geoffrey strode off towards the town.

Chapter Nine

The Signal

When Duclair left the cliff he hurried back to town. He did not even look round to see if Cartland was still following him. He crossed Bridge Street and walked fast down the lane to the Manor House. Once inside he felt safer.

Henley was reading in the library and enjoying a pipe.

'I beg your pardon, sir,' said Duclair. The way he emphasised the 'sir' annoyed the Squire. 'Have you seen Geoffrey?'

'No. I believe he's out. Is it time for his lessons?'

'Very nearly. I trust he will not be late.'

Henley grunted and returned his gaze to the book.

Duclair decided to remain in the Squire's presence. If the children were found at the foot of the cliff, and if by ill chance questions were asked of him. . . Well, it would be as well to have an alibi as far as possible.

He climbed a set of small curved steps which were used for reaching the upper bookshelves. His hands were trembling as he took down a book. Geoffrey had cried out a warning. Could he have seen his tutor on the clifftop? No, that would have been impossible. No one could have seen him . . . except Cartland of course. But Cartland was an ally.

His thoughts were interrupted by Henley. 'I hear you've been calling on the Annings.'

The book which Duclair was holding nearly slipped out of his hands. In spite of his effort to appear calm his voice came out loud and harsh. 'How – how did you—?' He cleared his throat. 'How did you know?'

Henley smiled. 'No one goes anywhere in this town without everyone knowing. Mrs Bell's sister saw you leaving the shop.'

Duclair thought rapidly. 'Yes, that's quite right. Of course I went there – to make sure that Cartland is not a spy.'

He was pleased with his neat reply. But no sooner had he congratulated himself than he happened to glance out of the library window. His heart began pounding again.

There, among the bushes, was Cartland – making his way towards the back of the house!

'*Mon Dieu!*' gasped Duclair, under his breath.

Henley was tapping his pipe out. 'And is he a spy?'

Duclair forced his attention back to Henley. 'A spy? Oh – no, Monsieur! Certainly not! A false alarm entirely!'

Henley nodded. 'Well, that's a relief, isn't it?' He looked up as Mrs Bell came in. 'Yes? What is it?'

'There's been a fox among the chickens,' said Mrs Bell. 'James said I should tell you—'

Henley rose. 'Another fox? How did it get in? I'd better see for myself!'

He left the room and Mrs Bell followed him.

Duclair wiped perspiration from his brow and turned to the window again. There was no sign of Cartland now. Where had he gone? What was he doing there at all?

A voice spoke behind him. 'Monsieur!'

Duclair swung round. Cartland was standing in an opening at the end of the room, framed by two pillars.

'I wish to speak with you!' It sounded like a threat.

'Not here!' hissed Duclair in an urgent whisper. 'Go back – quickly!'

In his anxiety Duclair hurled himself at Cartland, pushing him back through the opening.

Beyond the opening was a small conservatory, a little room with glass walls where Henley kept a collection of plants. It had a glass-panelled door leading to the garden. Cartland had come in that way.

Once they were out of the library Duclair turned and pulled a pair of curtains that hung across the opening behind them.

'Those children might have been killed!' said Cartland. Though he spoke softly his voice showed his anger.

'Were they hurt?'

'No, they were not, as far as I could see. But you meant them to be—'

'I meant to frighten them, that is all. To scare them away from the beach! Did you know they were searching for something? Suppose they were to find the papers?'

Cartland spoke through clenched teeth. 'They are not looking for papers! The girl is looking for fossils.' Mrs Anning had told him about Mary's new occupation.

Duclair was getting angry now. Cartland had no right to accuse him like this! 'Whatever they are looking for, they are a danger to us. The boy – do you know who he is?'

Cartland was silent.

'He's my pupil, Geoffrey Turnstall – the one who saw you arrive!'

Cartland paused for a moment, taking this in. Then he returned to the attack. 'In that case you should leave him to me. I know how to handle these matters. I have been trained for this work. You, Monsieur – you are a blundering amateur!'

Duclair's head snapped back as if Cartland had struck him. His face went scarlet. 'How dare you!' In his rage his voice became louder. 'How dare you speak to me – *le Vicomte de Grenoble*—'

'Be quiet!' hissed Cartland. 'Someone will hear you!'

Duclair stopped, but his face remained burning red.

'Show me where the papers are hidden!' whispered Cartland. 'After that you can leave everything to me!'

'No! I will leave nothing to you!'

There was a moment's silence. Duclair knew it was his duty to hand over the papers but he could not bring himself to do it. 'You shall see the papers when the boat comes to fetch you,' he continued. 'Until then you can wait!'

The look of anger on Cartland's face gave Duclair much satisfaction. It was then they heard a voice from the library.

'Monsieur Duclair—?'

It was Geoffrey.

Cartland turned at once and went out of the conservatory to the garden. Duclair watched him go, then shut the conservatory door as if he had just walked in. He pushed back the curtains and went into the library.

'Oh, there you are, Monsieur,' said Geoffrey.

'Er – yes. I was waiting in the garden. . . .' Duclair felt strangely pleased with himself. Obviously Geoffrey had not seen him on the cliff, so that was all right. And he felt he had won a victory over Cartland. He picked up his cane and swung it. 'We shall start our lesson. Arithmetic, is it not?'

Geoffrey was not interested in arithmetic just then.

'Monsieur! I've seen him again! Cartland! He was on the clifftop. And would you believe it? He pushed a rock on top of me. At least he tried to!'

'Come, come, now!' said Duclair. 'What are you talking about?'

As Geoffrey told the story Duclair weighed it in his mind. So he was not suspected, but Cartland was! He had a curious desire to laugh.

'Did you actually see him pushing the rock?' he asked when Geoffrey had finished.

'Of course not, but—'

'Ah! I thought as much. A rock fell. Mr Cartland happened to be walking past. No doubt he heard it fall and he came forward, very properly, to see if anyone had been hurt—'

'No, no!' Geoffrey was desperate. 'I'm sure he pushed it! He must have done!'

'Your uncle is quite right, boy. You have a fevered imagination.'

'But I tell you—'

'Silence!' Duclair rapped the cane on Henley's desk. 'You will not accuse an innocent man in this way! If you speak to your uncle about it, he will be angry too. You know that, don't you? Now get your books. And forget about Cartland!'

Geoffrey went to fetch his arithmetic book. But he could not forget. . .

Mary put her chisel to a rock. Her hammer rose and fell. When the rock split there was nothing inside it. She threw the pieces aside and stared out to the sea. For days now she had found nothing interesting – ever since Geoffrey had poured his scornful words over her, 'There are no monsters . . . you're just a silly little girl. . . .' Geoffrey was a rich boy with clever people to teach him. Surely he must know better than her? Perhaps he was right. Perhaps she was wasting her time.

'Yah–hah!' came a yell from the cliff.

Two ragged lads from the town were standing at the top, looking down at her and grinning.

One of them threw his head back and began to sing in a tuneless voice:

> 'Mary, Mary, quite contrary,
> How does your garden grow?
> With serpent stones and verterbries,
> And crocodiles all in a row!'

Then they burst out laughing.

Mary's hands froze on the tools she was holding. Of course everyone in town knew about her. The little girl with big ideas! Fancying herself as a fossil-hunter! Exploring a world that never was, for monsters that didn't exist. Oh, it was very funny. . .

The boys' laughter still floated back to her as they wandered to the road out of sight.

Mary forced the hammer to the chisel again, but tears were running down her cheeks.

It was about ten o'clock that night when the light first became visible, winking on and off, far out at sea. No one in the town was likely to have noticed it, except the man who was keeping watch.

Night after night Cartland had sat at the window of his room, his eyes on the sea. Now his vigil was rewarded.

He moved quickly to the chest of drawers on which his storm lantern stood, ready primed with oil. He drew sparks from his tinder box to light the wick. The flame grew slowly. He shut the little glass door at the side of the lantern and carried it to the window. He drew it slowly across the window from side to side and back again.

After a few moments the light at sea disappeared. After a pause it appeared again, remaining shining steadily for a count of ten, then disappeared altogether.

Cartland answered with a similar signal, holding his light steady while he counted ten. Then he blew it out.

He took his hat and cloak and went down the stairs. He knew where to look for Duclair. He had received a note, unsigned. It said simply, 'The Assembly Rooms, every night after dark.'

There was a stiff breeze blowing as he crossed the square. The breeze worried him a little. He hoped it would not get any stronger.

Duclair was sitting in the billiard room, watching a game and very bored with it. He made no sign as Cartland sat in a chair beside him. Both kept their eyes on the game.

'The boat is on its way.'

Duclair nodded.

'I will meet you on the beach . . . about midnight,' Cartland added.

Duclair nodded again.

Cartland watched the game a little longer, as if that was what he had come for, then got up and strolled out.

He went back to his room. There would be another signal telling him when the boat was about to land. He sat in front of the window and waited for it as patiently as he could.

The breeze did grow stronger. It became a wind which picked at the window of Geoffrey's bedroom, drew it wide open and slammed it shut again. Bang . . . bang. . .

Geoffrey was uneasily asleep, dreaming of French cannon-balls firing at him. Then it became a window banging near his head and he was awake. He dragged himself out of bed and the window jerked wide open as he reached for it.

Black clouds had gathered, blotting out the moonlight. The wind tugged at his hair and felt icily cold. He decided there was going to be a storm, and shuddered. He leaned still further out to grasp the window catch. And then he saw the light. It was out at sea, but not very far out. It was winking, on and off.

Geoffrey's thoughts began to race. The time must be near to midnight. Why should a light be winking. . . ? Suddenly the winking stopped. For a moment there was nothing, then the light appeared again for several seconds. At last it went out for good.

A signal! Geoffrey was sure it must be a signal of some sort, from a boat at sea. A signal for Cartland? Who else? A boat had brought him. Was it coming to take him back again?

The questions buzzed in his head as he dressed.

When he reached the hall downstairs he heard voices from the sitting room. His uncle was entertaining some guests. He wanted to go in and tell them all. . . But he knew it was no use doing that. His uncle would say that he had imagined the light. He would be made to look a fool in front of everyone again.

He took his cloak from the closet. Since no one would listen to him he must investigate on his own. At least he would prove to himself that he was right. He knew it was brave of him to go out alone and he felt proud of his own courage.

When he left the house he felt a lash of rain in his face. This would do his chest no good! No matter! He recalled the famous message of Lord Nelson to his fleet before the Battle of Trafalgar. 'England expects every man will do his duty. . .' Nelson wouldn't have cared about a weak chest.

Geoffrey pressed forward into the growing storm. . .

Chapter Ten

The Night of the Storm

The rain was falling heavily, whipped about by the wind, as Duclair clambered from the beach on to the ledge under Black Ven cliffs. The water was eating into the rock. It melted the surface of the ancient mud and made it very slippery. Duclair stepped carefully. He did not want to fall and smear his clothes with mud. That might be difficult to explain later.

It was also very dark. Only the jagged edge of the cliff above, a faint outline through the rain, gave him an idea of his position. At last he felt coarse grass under his feet and breathed a sigh of relief. Not far to go now.

He stepped down into the grassy hollow. He was several minutes feeling about for the old smugglers' cask. A panic seized him. Had someone removed it? Had they found—? Then he stumbled over it in the darkness, and just saved himself from falling. He tipped the cask aside. Beneath it was a cavity in the rock. Tucked into the cavity was an oilskin packet. Duclair took it out and put the cask back in its place.

The packet was dripping with water, but the papers wrapped inside it would be dry. He shook the packet to get rid of as much wetness as possible, then stuffed it into a pocket inside his coat.

When he stepped out of the hollow again he saw the light of a lantern. It was moving slowly towards him along the beach. He cupped his hands to his mouth and shouted.

'Captain Peronne! This way! Up here!'

The wind was so strong it seemed to blow his voice back into his throat. Nevertheless it must have carried far enough, for the light changed direction. It bobbed up on to the ledge. A few moments later Cartland was at his side.

'You have the papers, Monsieur?'

Duclair did not answer. 'Where is the boat?' he asked instead.

'They gave another signal. They are coming in to land. You can give me the papers now.'

Whatever Duclair might have said was interrupted by a sudden squall of wind which threatened to blow both men down on the slippery rock. They staggered, and waited till they could speak again.

'I do not see any light!' shouted Duclair. He was looking out to sea.

Cartland followed his gaze. Each man had the same thought in his mind. The wind had doubled in strength since the last signal from the boat. Even in the darkness white foam caps could be seen on the waves, dancing two or three feet high only a few yards from the shore. Could any boat risk landing in such conditions? Rocks were strewn under the shallow sea close to the beach. Raised by the waves and dropped again, a boat could easily be split open.

Suddenly the whole scene of sea and sky was brightly lit by a jagged flash of lightning.

'Now!' cried Duclair. 'Do you see—?'

There was nothing to be seen.

Another squall followed the lightning flash and carried thunder with it.

When the roar had died away, Duclair spoke. 'The boat has turned back. It is no wonder. They cannot land in this!'

Cartland's face looked white and strained in the light of the lantern. 'They will wait till the wind dies. Then they will try again.'

Duclair shook his head. 'If they value their lives they will make for France. That is the only shelter open to them. Pray God they get there safely.' He looked at Cartland. 'They will not come tonight!'

Cartland gritted his teeth. 'They must! They are ordered! I will wait till morning. There is no need for you to stay too. Give me the papers.'

'No!' Another flash of lightning lit the ledge. Duclair's face was set in a stubborn line under the rainwater which trickled over it. 'You shall not have those papers till I see the boat!'

Cartland was breathing heavily. The rain had washed his hair down over his eyes and he looked savage. 'Boat or no boat, Monsieur—' His words were drowned in thunder and he waited till it had died away. 'I'll not have you play games with me. Give me the papers!'

He leaned forward as he spoke and Duclair took a step backward. For the first time he was actually afraid. But he shook his head.

Cartland's fist shot out. His fingers clutched the cloak where it was tied under Duclair's chin. He fastened it in a grip of steel.

'Let me go—! How dare you—?' Duclair struggled in vain.

'The papers! If you do not hand them over . . .' His grip tightened still further. His knuckles pressed into the other man's throat. Duclair gave a frightened gasp.

It was then they heard the scream. . . .

Geoffrey had felt the full blast of the storm when he left the sheltered lane that led from the Manor House. Out on the turnpike road high above the beach the wind tore at his cloak as if it were a sail, threatening to blow him off his feet. The rain beat at his face like cats' claws. It seeped under his collar and slowly soaked him to the skin.

In spite of it all he kept going. He guessed from the distance he had walked that he must be above Black Ven. He turned off the road, moving cautiously towards the edge of the cliff. He could see nothing. He hardly dared take another step forward.

The first flash of lightning came to his aid. It showed him the cliff edge only a few yards away. He bent down on hands and knees for safety, and crawled towards the edge. He peered over and gave a gasp of triumph.

There was the light of a lantern on the ledge far below. It was a poor light in such a huge darkness but it showed a tall man holding it. Cartland, of course. . . . And beside him – another man! A good deal smaller than Cartland. . . . That was all Geoffrey could make out. But one thing was sure. There was a second spy! If only he could see them both, clearly. . . . To do that he would have to go down to the beach.

Geoffrey remembered the ravine. It could only be a few yards away, further along the cliff. He began to make his way towards it, moving just far enough away from the cliff edge to keep it in sight as a guideline.

There was more lightning and another clap of thunder. The wind screamed in his ears. In a way he was glad of the storm. Once on the beach he could get quite close to the men without risk of being seen or heard. He must only keep his head down if the lightning flashed.

A gap appeared right in his path. The ravine! Carefully he lowered himself over the edge.

What Geoffrey had not allowed for was the effect of the rain on the loose shale that covered the slope. Water was pouring down the ravine as if through a funnel. It carried some of the shale with it, while the rest became soaked into a slippery sludge.

As soon as Geoffrey's feet touched the slope they slid away from under him. He was rushing downward between the narrow walls at a speed which increased with every yard. There was nothing to hold on to, no grip for his boots. He screamed. . . .

At the sound of the scream Cartland relaxed his grip on Duclair, who took another step back, panting.

The scream was followed by cries. 'Help! Help!'

The voice was familiar to Duclair. 'The boy!' he exclaimed. 'Geoffrey!'

Cartland was already striding towards the sound. After a few steps he paused. The cries had stopped. A squall of wind passed and then he heard another sound, more like a groan.

Geoffrey was lying at the foot of the slope. He sat up. To his surprise he was quite unhurt. His fall had been slowed down by the pile of muddy shale at the bottom, on which he now lay.

The lantern came swinging in front of his eyes. He gave a cry of fresh fear and rose to his feet. Before he could run a big hand closed over his shoulder.

'Got you, my boy!' Cartland's voice roared in his ears like the thunder itself. 'You have interfered once too often!'

Another flash of lightning lit their faces. Cartland's expression was terrible to see. The thunder crashed almost over their heads.

Geoffrey thought he was going to be murdered on the spot. It seemed so certain that for a moment he was too numb even to feel terror.

Then the hand on his shoulder yanked him round and started shoving him along the ledge. Geoffrey dared not speak and Cartland said nothing. His face, lit by the lantern, had become wooden.

They reached the spot where Duclair had been standing. Cartland raised the lantern. There was no one there! Duclair had seized his chance and escaped!

Geoffrey felt the grip tighten even further on his shoulder and he gave a cry of pain. Then they were moving forward once more. Geoffrey knew they were heading for the town....

There was no one left on the beach. The rain was still beating down the cliffs. It ran down the face of the rock in tiny rivulets which met together and became cascades of water. Running streams from the cliffs washed over the ledges below. The streams swept away the shale and dug into the muddy rock like liquid spades. Harder stones were left jutting out.

At last the thunder was beginning to die away, but a last flash of lightning lit up the work of the storm. It lit the new channels that had been scarred into the rock. It lit a blunt, stone-like snout that now rose an inch or two above the surface of the ledge. It seemed to be sniffing the air, as if the monster below were trying to escape.

Chapter Eleven

The Jail

Everyone in the Manor House was in bed when Duclair returned. He had hurried back from the beach as fast as he could. He was afraid that Cartland might be after him. Duclair let himself in through the conservatory door and closed it thankfully against the wind and rain.

The fire still burned in the library and he stood shivering in front of it. When at last he felt the warmth through his wet clothes he sat down in the winged armchair. He was desperately tired. He longed to get into a dry bed, but he dared not do so yet. Duclair dreaded the sound of an angry thump on the conservatory door. What he would do if Cartland came he had no idea. Meanwhile he waited and the warmth seeped further into his chilled body. . . .

Next morning Henley was down almost before it was light. Mrs Bell went out to the yard, calling to the stableman.

'See that Bessie is harnessed,' she ordered. 'The Squire is leaving in a few minutes.'

Henley did not enjoy his breakfast. Nothing tasted well at such an early hour. Mrs Bell helped him put on his heavy travelling cloak.

'All is ready for you, sir,' she said.

'I have some business papers to take with me,' said Henley. 'On my desk ... I'll fetch them myself. No need to fuss, woman. You can get on with your work.'

Mrs Bell retired to the kitchen quarters and Henley went into the library. He was half-way to his desk when he saw Duclair, fast asleep in the big armchair.

His legs were spread-eagled. His hat was still on his head, tipped over at a rakish angle. His clothes, usually so neat, were crumpled. There was mud splashed on his trouser legs.

'Duclair!' exclaimed Henley.

The Frenchman woke with a startled gasp. 'Oh! *Mon Dieu!* Where am I?' He looked round in astonishment. Henley was staring at him, suspicious. 'I – I must have fallen asleep. I came in – er – rather late. I was very weary. . . .' He took his hat off and tried to blink the sleep out of his eyes.

'I quite understand,' said Henley.

Duclair blinked again. Understand? What did Henley understand?

'Too much drink, eh?' Henley smiled as he went to his desk and sorted out the papers he was looking for. 'I'm told you've been down at the Assembly Rooms every night. Well, well – we all have to relax a bit sometimes.'

Duclair rose to his feet unsteadily. He was about to protest in anger. How dare anyone accuse *him* (*le Vicomte de Grenoble!*) of coming home drunk! On second thoughts he decided to hold his tongue. Henley was satisfied with the explanation, and Duclair had nothing better to offer.

'I apologise!' he said at last.

Henley was no longer interested. 'I'm going to Charmouth. I shall be back this afternoon. Please tell Geoffrey I could not wait for him.'

Geoffrey! Duclair remembered the cry for help. What had happened to Geoffrey?

'Is he – er – have you seen him this morning—?'

Henley shook his head. 'Mrs Bell knocked on his door an hour ago but he didn't answer. He must be still asleep. I promised to take him to Charmouth with me, but if he can't get up in time it's his own fault. Tell him I had to go without him.'

'Yes. Of course. I will tell him.'

Henley went out to the hall and Duclair sank back in the chair with relief.

There were sounds in the yard. Bessie stamping on the flagstones and Sappho barking. Then the noise of hooves trotting. So Henley was away. . . .

Duclair gripped the arms of the chair. He must think of everything calmly, step by step. The first thing was the oilskin packet in his coat. He must find a new hiding place for the papers. That problem was easily solved. He went to one of the library shelves, chose a large book and took it down. He put the packet on the shelf at the back, then replaced the book.

The next step was to go upstairs to Geoffrey's room. He pushed the door open and looked in. There was no sign of Geoffrey. Much as he disliked the idea, Duclair knew that he must contact Cartland again as soon as possible, and find out what he had done with the boy.

Geoffrey's first feelings when he woke up were of cold and stiffness. Something was tickling his nose. It was straw. Just ahead of him was a patch of early-morning sunlight. The patch was criss-crossed by long, thin shadows. He forced his aching muscles to work in order to look up. The shadows came from a window set high in the wall, criss-crossed by iron bars.

From outside came the faint sound of waves lapping on the beach.

Geoffrey sat up and began to cough. His clothes were still damp and his chest felt bad. He remembered the nightmare walk along the beach with Cartland, then a dark passage and the sensation of being thrust into a pit. . . . He could see now that a couple of stone steps led down from a heavy, iron-studded door. When he was pushed into the room he had fallen down the steps.

He wanted to get up. He wanted to pound on the door (which was surely locked) and scream for help. But his legs would scarcely work. He began to stretch each limb, one after the other.

He was interrupted by a deep, throaty voice.

'Wake up, me lads!' it boomed.

There was a small barred opening set in the door. A face was peering through it. It was a large, round face with a stubble of beard and several unsightly warts. Shaggy black hair fell over the eyes. The lips parted in what was possibly meant to be a grin. Several teeth were missing and those that were left were a dark brown colour. Geoffrey decided it was the most unpleasant face he had ever seen.

There was a thump as an iron bolt was drawn back on the other side of the door, then the rattle of a key in the lock. The door opened and the owner of the face appeared. He was not tall, but very broad and muscular. A dirty kerchief was knotted round his neck. His shirt was ripped. His baggy breeches were held up by a thick leather belt with a big brass buckle. He was carrying a tin tray with a jug of water and a hunk of dark brown bread.

'Ready for our breakfast, are we?' he inquired as he came down the steps.

We? Geoffrey looked round but there was no one else to be seen.

'Who are you?' he asked.

'Peebles is the name. Jailers to the town of Lyme Regis, that's what we are.'

Jailer! So that's where he was – in the town jail!

Peebles put the tray on a rickety table. It had an old three-legged stool beside it. There was no other furniture.

Geoffrey climbed to his feet. 'Why am I—?' he began, and stopped as a fit of coughing overtook him. He leaned back against the wall till the spasm passed.

'Nasty cough we got there,' observed Peebles. 'Don't you go and fall sick. We won't have it, we won't.'

In spite of the 'we', Geoffrey knew there could only be one jailer. In fact there was probably only one cell and (at the moment) one prisoner – himself.

'What am I doing here?' Geoffrey managed to say.

'Well may you ask,' said Peebles, knitting his thick brows into a heavy frown.

'That man brought me here, last night!' said Geoffrey.

'Very right and proper too!' Peebles wagged a stubby finger at him. 'After you tried to steal his wallet.'

'I—!' gasped Geoffrey. 'I stole—?'

'Such wickedness!' Peebles shook his head sadly. 'We ought to be ashamed of ourselves, and that's a fact.'

'Did he tell you I'd stolen his wallet? He's lying! And d'you know why? Because he's a French spy. He's an agent of Napoleon Bonaparte. I have found him out!'

Peebles was nodding his head. 'French spies, is it? Well now, that's a new story. We never heard that one afore now.'

'It's true!'

'I warn you, me lads, if you go on saying things like that, you'll be had for slander as well as thieving!'

Geoffrey knew it was hopeless to argue. Peebles would take the word of a 'gentleman' like Cartland against his.

Geoffrey was coated from head to foot in the mud of Black Ven. The back of his cloak had been torn in the slide down the cliff. He looked like a ragamuffin from the streets.

He made a dive for the open door.

Peebles moved with a speed which was surprising in such a heavy man. His fist closed on Geoffrey's shoulder before the boy was half-way up the steps. Geoffrey felt himself yanked almost off his feet, and swung round till his face was only a few inches from the brown teeth and the warts. The smell of Peebles' breath made him feel sick.

'Them as comes here, stays here, till justice be done!' said Peebles. 'And that won't be till Friday at the earliest.'

He gave Geoffrey a thrust which sent him spinning on his back in the corner. Peebles went up the steps.

'Wait!' cried Geoffrey. 'You can't keep me here. I'm not a thief! My father is Sir Joshua Turnstall. He's a high official at the War Office.'

Peebles turned on the top step. His stomach began to shake with laughter. 'High official! Oh, that's rich, that is! The War Office, no less! And what be you, may we ask? Squire of the Parish, no doubt?'

'No, not me. That's my uncle!'

It sent Peebles into fresh spasms of laughter. 'Some real wags we have here and no mistake!'

Geoffrey felt tears of frustration in his eyes. 'I tell you it's true. Ask at the Manor House. Please!'

Peebles shook his head again. 'They think of some tales, they do, and that's a fact!'

He stumped out to the passage. The door slammed, the bolt ground home and the key turned in the lock.

Geoffrey ran up the steps and stood on tip-toe to peer through the grille. 'If I am telling the truth, think how you'll suffer for it. Think of that and go to the Manor House. Ask for the Squire's nephew. . . .'

There was no answer except Peebles' heavy footsteps going down the passage.

Cartland paced up and down at the Cobb. He chose the spot where he had met Duclair before, hoping that Duclair would come back to the same place. He breathed a sigh of relief as he saw the little man coming down the street from the town.

Duclair had changed his clothes and looked as dapper as ever. As soon as he reached Cartland he hissed, 'Well? What did you do with the boy?'

Cartland told him.

Duclair's hand trembled as he reached for his snuffbox. 'In the jail? How long do you think he will stay there? When they find out who he is—'

'I have paid the jailer to take good care of him,' answered Cartland. 'We need only one day. Tonight the boat will come again.'

Duclair glared at the nets strung out on the beach. 'You would have been wiser to throw him from the top of the cliff. No one would have seen you do it. People would have thought that the foolish boy fell over during the storm. You would have been safe then. And so would I!'

Cartland stiffened. 'I do not make war on children!'

Two fishermen passed and Cartland was silent until they had gone. 'I will meet you on the beach again tonight,' he said. He turned and marched away.

'Pray God it will still be possible,' muttered Duclair.

Duclair made his way back to the Manor House as fast as he could. He expected to find the servants in a panic. They must have found out that Geoffrey was missing. The news that the Squire's nephew had disappeared would spread quickly.

But there was no panic. Sarah, the parlourmaid, was dusting in the sitting room as usual.

'Where is Master Geoffrey?' Duclair asked her, wondering what she would reply.

'Why, sir, didn't you know? He's gone to Charmouth with the Squire.'

Duclair tried not to look surprised. 'Really? I thought he wasn't up in time. . . ?'

'He wasn't up in time for breakfast,' Sarah explained patiently. 'But when Mrs Bell went to his room she found he'd gone. His cloak was gone too. So he must have heard the Squire leaving and run downstairs just in time.'

'Ah! Quite so. . . .' Duclair breathed more easily. What a wonderful piece of luck! Geoffrey would not be missed after all – at least until Henley returned from Charmouth. If Henley were delayed, if he decided to stay in Charmouth overnight, all might be well. . . .

Chapter Twelve

One More Try

'Mary! Come along, dear! The sun's been risen an hour or more!' Mrs Anning called up the stairs.

'Coming, Mama. . . .'

Mary had slept later than usual after the storm. When she got down to the living room her porridge was on the table. The usual bundle of bread and cheese lay in its cloth on the dresser, beside the wallet of tools.

Mary did not know whether her mother still disapproved of her going down to the beach. Mrs Anning did not speak about it any more. Every morning she prepared Mary's breakfast and her lunch, just as she would for a son who went out to work.

Mary sat in front of the porridge but did not eat.

'What is the matter, dear?' asked her mother. 'Don't you want to get down to the beach as quickly as possible? That rain last night will have loosened the rocks. You should make some good finds today. Your father always said that the best time to search was after heavy rain.'

'Yes, I know. . .' she hesitated. 'Mama. . .'

'Yes?'

'People think I'm foolish, don't they? Mary Anning and her grand ideas! They laugh at me, I know they do!'

Mrs Anning frowned. 'It's none of their business.'

Mary looked up at her. 'But what if they're right? You said yourself it's not proper for the likes of me to work on the beach. You always told father it was a waste of time—'

'I – I may have said so—' Mrs Anning looked confused. She had not heard her daughter express doubts before. But then, Mary was only a child. Perhaps, like a child, she had tired of her new game.

As if Mary could read her mother's thoughts she suddenly cried out, 'They think I'm just a silly girl, playing a game! If only I could prove they're wrong! If I could find. . .' Her fists clenched in her eagerness. 'I could show those learned men a thing or two—'

'Oh, my lamb!' Mrs Anning clasped her hands in dismay. 'There you go again! More grand ideas! Always asking for the moon!'

Mary's eagerness left her. She spoke quietly. 'Very well. I'll not go to the beach any more. I'll learn to make lace. Then you'll be proud of me.'

'But Mary – I *am* proud of you!' Mrs Anning put an arm round her shoulder. 'It shows a brave spirit, to make up your mind what you want, and to go on trying for it – whatever people say!'

'Oh, Mama!' Mary embraced her.

Mrs Anning sighed. 'You'll not be happy if you give up. So just you go on trying. . . .'

Mary ate her porridge in a few quick gulps. She grabbed the tools and her lunch and gave her mother a grateful kiss.

'I don't care what anyone *else* thinks!' she said.

She walked down the beach by the water's edge till she

came to Black Ven, then she climbed on to her favourite ledge. The rock was still glistening wet and the surface was soft. She began looking for harder lumps that might contain well-preserved fossils.

After an hour or more she had found nothing exciting. She was disappointed. The doubts began to return. If she could not find fossils after a storm like that, when *would* she succeed?

It was then she heard footsteps. She was surprised to see Cartland climbing on to the ledge. He had just left Duclair at the Cobb.

'Good morning, Mary.' He smiled at her.

Mary rose and bobbed. 'Good morning, sir.'

'I wonder if you can help me. . . .' He chose his words carefully. 'I have lost some papers. I had them in my pocket and I think they must have fallen out. On the beach . . . around here somewhere. Have you ever noticed anything . . . in wrappings of some sort. . . ?' He felt sure that Duclair would have wrapped the documents to keep them dry.

Mary shook her head.

Cartland smiled again. 'No matter. I'll take a look for myself.'

He set off along the ledge towards the grassy patch where he had met Duclair during the night. Surely Duclair would have waited near the spot where the papers were hidden?

Mary knelt again. She heard his footsteps moving away. Suddenly he gave a gasp. She looked round. His foot had slipped on the wet rock. He flung out his arms to regain his balance. Then he moved on along the ledge.

Mary was about to return to her work when something caught her attention. Something which jutted out from the ledge at the spot where Cartland had slipped. Something wedge-shaped, blunt at the end, stone-like. . .

She kept her eyes fixed on the object, as though fearful that if she looked away for an instant it might disappear. She felt around her on the ledge till her hands found the tools. Then she rose and moved forward, step by step. At last she knelt. Scarcely breathing, she put out a finger and touched the grey stone. She knew at once it was fossil. The shape was different from anything she had seen before. The wedge was growing wider as it disappeared, suggesting more of it, much more, hidden under the shale. . .

Mary felt a thrill so strong it was almost like pain. She forced herself to sit back for a few moments till her breath came more evenly. She must be calm. She must take great care. She leaned forward again and began to move the loose pieces of shale with her bare fingers. Now and then she reached for the chisel, tapping very delicately. . .

Cartland looked round the grassy hollow. His eye fell on the old cask. He picked it up and looked at the hole in the ground where the cask had stood. There was nothing. He threw the cask aside angrily. He continued to search, kicking up tufts of grass in the hope of finding something underneath. The more he looked the more sure he became that he was wasting his time. Duclair had very likely taken the packet out of its hiding place before they met last night. In that case he had taken the papers with him. . . .

Cartland's thoughts were interrupted by a cry from Mary. He leapt out of the hollow and saw Mary kneeling. Her mud-blackened hands were pressed across her mouth as if to prevent herself from crying out again and again.

He hurried towards her. 'What is it, Mary? What's happened?'

She did not answer. She was staring down at the ledge in front of her.

He reached her side and looked down too. He blinked in amazement. 'Merciful heavens!'

He was staring at the forepart of a huge skull. The lower part of it was still clamped firmly in its bed of ancient rock, but Mary had uncovered the top. The wedge-shaped shout, several feet long, broadened out till it merged into a massive hump with a bony ridge in the middle. Either side of the ridge were two round, gaping holes. These must be eye-sockets! Though the eyes had long since disappeared the sockets themselves seemed to stare upward. . . .

Mary's voice came in a faint whisper. 'It's the crocodile! It must be!'

Cartland had never heard of the crocodile, but he nodded all the same.

Mary rose to her feet. However wonderful the find, this was no time to be frozen with awe. A great deal had to be done. 'I pray there may be more of it under the rock,' she said. 'The rest of the skull at least. And who knows, beyond that, the whole body of the creature!' She appealed to Cartland, 'Oh, sir! I can't possibly uncover it all on my own. Will you help me?'

Cartland shook his head. He too must be practical. 'I can't help you now. I have a more important matter to see to.'

'More important than this?' Mary could not imagine anything more important than the crocodile.

Cartland hesitated for a moment. The sightless eyes seemed to reproach him. Were those papers so important? Did battles and victories mean so much? This creature must have lain in the rock through every war in human history. What difference would it make – victory or defeat – in another thousand years?

He shook his head again, to clear such thoughts from his

99

mind. Of course victory mattered! Lord Wellington's dispatches mattered very much indeed.

'I'm sorry,' he said gently, and started back along the ledge.

Mary bit her lip. She was desperately eager to go on working, but her hands were already sore from shifting the shale and her arms were weary. She must have help! She climbed down from the ledge to the beach and set off towards the town.

Geoffrey was sipping water from the jug, hoping it was clean, when Peebles thrust his face at the grille in the door.

'Right, me lads! Any more sauce from you and we'll thrash you – that's a fact!'

'What—?'

'The Squires have gone to Charmouth today—'

'Oh, yes!' said Geoffrey, remembering. 'I know he was going, but—'

'And he's taken his nephews with him!'

'No!'

'Oh, yes, he has! I just met Mrs Bell, the housekeepers from the Manor – and she told me as much herself.' He stabbed a finger at Geoffrey through the grille. 'So that be all of that, and more'n enough!'

He marched off down the passage.

Geoffrey flung himself at the door. 'Uncle promised to take me but he didn't! I wasn't there! I'm here!'

Peebles' feet were clumping up the stairs to his own apartment above.

Geoffrey shrieked as loudly as he could, 'Let me out! I'll have the law on you! For wrongful arrest . . . and . . . kidnapping!'

The strain of shouting brought on another bout of coughing. When it died away he looked towards the window. It must overlook the beach, and there would be people on the beach.

He dragged the rickety table under the window and put the stool beside it. He climbed on to the table and could just see through the bars. The bathing huts were at the water's edge in front of him. People were strolling about.

Was it any use shouting? A dirty-looking prisoner screaming through the bars – who would listen to him?

Then a small figure came into view running along the beach towards the steps. Her bonnet askew, her cape billowing out behind her, her face streaked with mud.

'Mary!' he shouted.

She stopped, looking round.

'It's me! Geoffrey! Up here!'

Her face turned towards him and her eyes opened in amazement.

'Help me!' he cried.

She did not answer. She ran on towards the steps. . . .

Chapter Thirteen

'I'll Pay you Well!'

Geoffrey waited impatiently. At last there were footsteps in the passage and Peebles' voice boomed.

'We don't allow prisoners to be visited afore their trial . . . not as a rule, that is.'

Geoffrey leapt up the steps and squinted through the grille, trying to see along the passage. There was a faint chink of coins. Mary was pressing two sixpences into Peebles' hand. Peebles touched his forelock and his tone changed.

'But since you say you're a friend of his, there's maybe no harm, just this once.'

They came towards the door. Geoffrey stepped down as Peebles opened it. Mary came down the steps and the door closed after her.

'What are you doing here?' she asked.

She spoke fast, as if she wanted the business dealt with as quickly as possible.

Geoffrey was just as anxious as she was. All the same he paused before he answered. If he talked about Cartland she might get angry again. She might even refuse to believe him.

'A man brought me here. A man who wants me out of his way.'

'What man?' The question was snapped back at him.

'You – you wouldn't understand if I told you.'

'Is that so? I suppose I am too silly to understand? In that case, I don't see how I can help you!' She turned back to the door.

'Oh, no!' cried Geoffrey. 'I didn't mean that. You're not silly at all!' He bent his head and forced the next words through his lips. 'I'm sorry. About what I said to you on the beach. . . .'

He looked up. Mary was smiling. At first he thought she was enjoying her triumph, but when she spoke he realised there was more to it than that.

'That's all right,' she said. 'No one will think I'm silly ever again. No one will laugh any more. What do you want me to do?'

'Please explain to that jailer who I am!' begged Geoffrey.

He was afraid she would demand more explanations that would start another argument. But to his relief her sense of urgency had returned.

'Mr Peebles!' she called.

The door opened again at once. Peebles must have been listening just outside. He appeared at the top of the steps.

Mary began briskly. 'The man who brought this prisoner – how much did he pay you?'

Geoffrey was startled.

Peebles looked stricken with horror. 'Pay us!' he gasped. 'Now, Miss Anning, you know very well that we wouldn't take money from anyone—'

'How much?' insisted Mary.

Peebles sighed. 'Five pounds, it were.'

'What!' cried Geoffrey. Such a simple explanation had never occurred to him. Mary obviously knew the ways of the world – especially those of Lyme Regis – a lot better than he did.

Peebles went on hastily, 'Only to cover the cost of finding witnesses and suchlike.'

'Well,' said Mary, 'this young man's father is very rich indeed!'

Peebles began to look worried.

Mary continued, 'If he were to hire lawyers—'

Peebles raised his hands as if to ward off evil spirits. 'Oh, no, Miss! We don't want no lawyers—'

'Then you'd better think about it.' Mary delivered the final blow. 'His uncle is Squire Henley.'

There was silence.

Would Peebles believe it now? The look on his face gave the answer. Evidently he knew Mary well enough to be sure she would not lie to him. His eyes grew round as he breathed, 'Is that a fact? But Mrs Bell—'

'Mrs Bell was mistaken!' snorted Geoffrey, impatient. 'Uncle *meant* to take me with him, but he didn't!'

Peebles did not answer. His mouth had dropped open.

Geoffrey turned to Mary, 'Thank you very much,' he said.

Suddenly Peebles stepped forward. He grabbed Geoffrey's right hand in his own two hairy paws and shook it up and down. 'My good sirs!' he declared in the friendliest tones he could manage. ''Tis an honour to meet you!'

Geoffrey snatched his hand away and strode up the steps to the open door.

Peebles called after him anxiously. 'Just taking care of you, we was – till we found out who you were—'

But Geoffrey was gone.

Peebles turned to Mary, still anxious. 'Tell the Squires as how we meant no harm.'

Mary nodded absently. Now that Geoffrey's problem was solved her thoughts were already back with the crocodile. An idea had occurred to her.

'Mr Peebles, have you any other prisoners to look after today?'

'Why no, Miss. Trade's a bit slack as you might say.' He chuckled at his own joke.

'But you want to earn money, don't you?'

Peebles nodded eagerly.

'Very well. You can earn some money, if you help me....'

Half an hour later a curious procession started along the beach from Lyme, heading for Black Ven.

In front was the small figure of Mary. Behind her were Peebles and three more men, all equally ill-dressed and unshaven. They carried spades and shovels over their shoulders and looked like a squad of ragged soldiers marching after an undersized leader.

Mary had asked Peebles to gather a work-gang for her. He had clearly chosen them from among the petty thieves who occupied his jail from time to time – perhaps the only friends he had.

She had no fear of them. They might be thieves, but they were not cut-throats. And anyhow, she thought grimly, they would find it very difficult to steal the crocodile.

They passed Cartland who was on his way back to town after his useless search. He paused to look at the odd group, and nodded to Mary. She nodded back and strode on.

At last they reached the ledge.

'There is the creature!' she said, pointing to what could be seen of it. 'I hope we shall find much more of it. We cannot dig it out of the rock just yet. That will be a long job, and a slow one. I want you to help me uncover the top of it, so that we can see what there is.'

There was no reply. She looked round. The men were staring at the skull with their mouths open.

Peebles was the first to find words. 'Pity on our souls!' he gasped.

Mary sank to her knees and ran her fingers over the skull, as one might stroke a pet dog. 'Isn't he beautiful?' she said.

The others did not seem to think so. They hung back as if loath to come any nearer.

'Why, Miss Anning, that be a terrible monster!' said one of them who was known as Big Jim.

A small man with a patch over one eye made the sign of the cross over his chest to ward off evil. ''Tis no work for good Christians, the likes of us!'

He turned away and began to march back along the ledge. Big Jim shook his head sadly and also turned away. The fourth man, a stupid-looking fellow, followed the other two.

Mary rose to her feet in dismay and appealed to Peebles. 'Don't let them go!'

Peebles looked none too sure himself, but he called after them, 'Come back here! Would you have the young girls think us a bunch of cowards?'

They stopped. Big Jim shouted back. 'She's got no fear, that one. On account of the lightning that struck her. She's got electric fluid in her veins. 'Tis different for us!'

They started moving away again.

Mary shouted. ''Tis naught to do with lightning! There's naught to be afraid of. Whatever the creature is, God made him like any other. Would you be afraid of God's own work?'

The men paused again. Mary followed up her advantage with a more practical argument. 'I'll pay you well, I promise!'

The three put their heads together.

'How will you get the money?' asked Big Jim.

'When I sell it, of course,' Mary answered promptly. 'I'll get ten, twenty pounds or more for this!'

Twenty pounds! The girl would be rich! Big Jim nodded and came back towards her. The other two followed him reluctantly.

'That's better, me lads,' said Peebles. 'Now we can get to work. Use your spades to loosen the rock, then shovel it off.'

By way of example Peebles raised his own spade. He was about to bring it straight down into the rock on top of the crocodile.

'Not that way!' cried Mary. She grasped his raised arm before he could lower it. 'You'll damage the bones underneath. You must take the rock off sideways, across the top, a little bit at a time.' She took the spade to show them what she meant, though it was so heavy she could hardly wield it. 'The creature must not be hurt, not one little bit. . . .'

One by one the men took their positions in a line beyond the skull. The crunch of spades in the soft rock began to be heard.

Mary knelt beside the skull. She took her brush from the toolbag and began to clean away the mud which still clung to it. The mud had dried in the sunlight and now it came away in little flurries of dust.

They had not been long at work when the small man with the patch squinted along the beach with his one good eye and pointed.

'What be this?' he asked.

They all looked up. Mary rose to her feet.

Some young boys were leaping and scampering along the beach towards the ledge. Beyond them were more people, and beyond them more still. In twos and threes they were dotted along the beach as far back as the town itself. Several were visitors, others were townsfolk. There were young and old, ladies and gentlemen of fashion, and workpeople in their working clothes. A strange assortment to see on the beach all at the same time. But they all had a common aim. They were heading for Black Ven. . . .

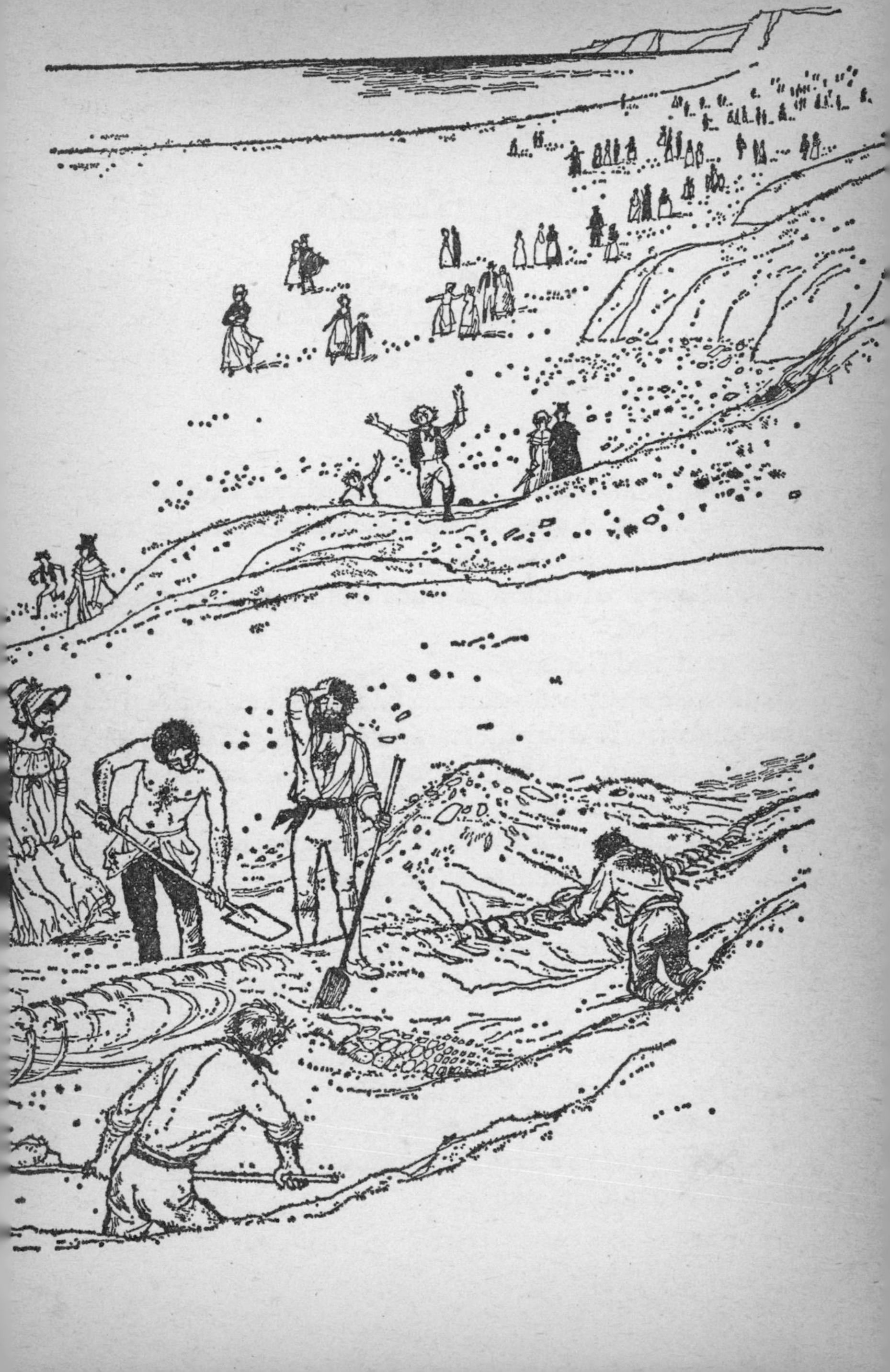

Chapter Fourteen

The Other Spy

Freed from jail, Geoffrey made for the Manor House. Now they would have to listen to him! He threw open the front door and marched into the hall.

Duclair appeared almost at once from the sitting room. 'You!' he gasped.

'Yes, me!' said Geoffrey.

Now that he had such a startling tale to tell he was prepared to take it slowly, to enjoy the full effect. He ripped off his torn cloak and threw it with his hat on to a chair. Then he strode past Duclair into the sitting room.

Duclair's face was as white as chalk. He put a hand inside his coat and drew out his snuffbox. 'Have you – er – have you just come back from Charmouth?'

Geoffrey stood, legs apart, in front of the fireplace the way his uncle often did. 'I haven't been to Charmouth,' he said slowly. 'I've been to jail.'

He expected more reaction from Duclair who simply raised his hand to his nose to sniff the powder.

'Don't you believe me?' asked Geoffrey.

Duclair snapped the lid of the snuffbox shut. 'You'd better tell me all about it,' he said.

Geoffrey told his story carefully, from the moment he had seen the signal out at sea, and had set off to investigate.

Duclair sat in a chair and listened without interrupting. His face was still white. It showed no expression at all.

'If it hadn't been for Mary I might have been in jail all week!' Geoffrey concluded.

'How fortunate you were able to escape,' said Duclair, thought his voice did not sound cheerful. 'And Cartland ... have you seen him again?'

'Of course not. I ran straight back here.'

'Yes. That was very wise of you. You were wise to come to me.'

'You've got to do something at once. Uncle isn't here, so it's up to you.'

Duclair rose from his chair. 'You are right! I must do something! Cartland must be arrested!'

'Let us go now!' said Geoffrey. He was making for the door.

'*You* will not go anywhere. You will wait here!'

'Oh, but, please—'

'I cannot allow it! I am responsible for you while your uncle is away. Do you realise that if Cartland set eyes on you again, he might kill you? You are the witness to what he has done! You must stay here, out of harm's way!'

'Oh, very well!' Geoffrey was disappointed.

Duclair went out to the hall and put on his cloak and top hat. 'I advise you not to speak to anyone else about this,' he said, 'we can't be sure whom we can trust. Promise me you'll say nothing to anyone.'

Geoffrey nodded agreement.

Duclair looked satisfied. 'I suggest you change your clothes. And for heaven's sake, boy, wash that mud off your face!'

A few minutes later Duclair was walking down Bridge Street. He stopped at the Annings' shop. He glanced at the sign over the door. It had been changed from *Richard Anning, Carpenter* to *Mary Anning, Curiosities*. The bell tinkled over the door as he went in.

Mrs Anning came from the living room. 'Good morning, sir?'

'Good morning, ma'am,' said Duclair. 'If I might just look round . . . ?'

'By all means, sir. You are most welcome.' There had not been many customers and Mrs Anning was anxious to please.

He moved round the shop slowly. Mary's harvest from the beach was spread out rather thinly. Coloured shells and pebbles lay in trays on the old table. Several small fossils and some large shells were set out on the shelves. Duclair took his time, examining each object. He was listening for any sound from Cartland's room.

'Would you like some shells, sir?' asked Mrs Anning. 'You can make such pretty ornaments with shells. Like this.' She picked up a wooden box which had been decorated with shells of different colours and sizes.

'Yes. Very pretty, ma'am,' said Duclair. There was no sound in the house. Perhaps Cartland had gone out.

He was wondering what to do next when the street door opened and the man he was looking for came in.

Cartland stopped on seeing Duclair.

Duclair handed the box back to Mrs Anning. 'I will certainly look at the shells,' he said.

Then a man's voice was heard through the open doorway. It was someone calling across the square. 'Come on – down to the beach, quickly!'

'What's going on?' asked another voice.

'It's Mary Anning,' shouted the man. 'They say she's found a monster in the rocks!'

Mrs Anning drew in her breath. 'Mercy! Did you hear that—?' She turned to Duclair. 'Will you pardon me, sir, for just a moment—?'

Duclair nodded his head graciously and Mrs Anning hurried out to the street. Cartland closed the door after her.

'Well, Monsieur?'

'Geoffrey is free again!'

Cartland stiffened.

Duclair picked a shell out of the tray and examined it. He was not nervous any more. It actually gave him pleasure to see Cartland at a disadvantage. 'So much for your idea of putting him in jail.'

'Where is he?'

'I left him at the Manor House. He thinks I have come here to arrest you.'

There was silence. There was nothing Cartland could say.

Duclair put the shell back in the tray and turned to him. 'You must leave the town at once. You cannot wait for the boat to fetch you. Hire a horse at the inn and make for London. We have agents there, at the docks. They will arrange a passage for you on a neutral ship, to get you out of the country. That is the usual way of escape, I believe. But I am sure you know that, since you are so well trained.'

Cartland ignored the jibe. 'What about the papers?' he asked.

'You cannot take them with you. As soon as you are safely gone I shall have to raise a hue and cry. You will be a hunted man. I must find other means to send the papers to Paris.'

'Do you think you can carry on, just as before?'

'Why not? I shall say that you escaped before I could stop you. I suggest you make haste!'

Duclair went to the door just as Mrs Anning returned from the street. He bowed to her as he went out.

Mrs Anning raised her hands in a flutter as she spoke to Cartland. 'Oh, sir! Everyone in town is making for the beach. Can it be true? Has Mary really found—?'

Cartland interrupted her. 'Pray excuse me, ma'am. I have to leave at once!'

Geoffrey had washed and changed his clothes. He felt hungry. He went to the sitting room and pulled the bell cord.

There was no answer. The Manor servants, like the rest of the townspeople and visitors, were hurrying along the beach to Black Ven cliffs.

Geoffrey was puzzled. He went to the kitchen quarters but there was no one there. He helped himself to bread and beef from the larder.

It was a relief when he heard someone coming in at the front door. He ran to the hall. It was Duclair.

Geoffrey forgot the absent servants.

'Did you find Cartland? Is he caught?' he asked excitedly.

Duclair shook his head sadly. 'It is very unfortunate. He must have found out that you had escaped from the jail. He has gone!'

'Gone?' Geoffrey was bitterly disappointed. 'Gone where?'

Duclair shrugged his shoulders. 'Who can tell?' He took off his cloak.

'Have you told the Magistrate? Or the Revenue men? I believe there is an army camp, not far from the town—'

'Keep calm, my boy, keep calm!' Duclair pushed open the double doors of the library and went in.

More Beaver Books

We hope you have enjoyed this Beaver Book. Here are some of the other titles:

The Glass Knife Gripping and intriguing story about a boy who has been reared to become a human sacrifice. Set in South America before the European discovery of the New World; by John Tully, with illustrations by Victor Ambrus

The Worst Kids in the World The Sunday school Christmas pageant turned out to be very different from usual the year the Herdmans bagged all the star parts. Judith Gwyn Brown's illustrations accompany Barbara Robinson's funny yet sensitive story

Animal Quiz Johnny Morris, universally known and loved for his television programme *Animal Magic*, has created a picture quiz book about all sorts of animals, fish and birds, full of fun and fact for all the family

Midshipman Quinn The Napoleonic Wars are the setting for the adventures of Septimus Quinn and the frigate *Althea*, narrated by Showell Styles

Merlin's Mistake Brian, Maude and Tertius (Tertius is Merlin's 'mistake' because he was given the gift of all future knowledge in error) set out on a quest which leads them through many adventures, both dangerous and funny, to an unexpected but satisfying conclusion. By Robert Newman, author of *The Twelve Labours of Hercules*, also in Beavers

The Tower and the Traitors The amazing stories of just some of the men and women who have lived and died in the Tower of London; told by Barbara Leonie Picard

New Beavers are published every month and if you would like the *Beaver Bulletin* – which gives all the details – please send a large stamped envelope to:

Beaver Bulletin
The Hamlyn Group
Astronaut House
Feltham
Middlesex TW14 9AR

31958X